THE DAISY CHAIN

THE DAISY CHAIN

PREQUEL TO THE COLE EDWARDS SAGA

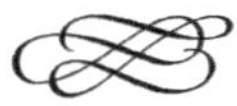

ERICA M. GOROS

Published by Death Do We Party Press

www.deathdoweparty.com

ISBNs:

Kindle: 979-8-9990532-6-8

Paperback: 979-8-9990532-4-4

Hardcover: 979-8-9990532-5-1

eBook: 979-8-9990532-3-7

Audiobook: 979-8-9990532-7-5

Cover design by Erica M. Goros

Interior design by Erica M. Goros

Printed in the United States of America

Content Advisory:

This book contains violence and sexual content. It is intended for mature readers.

When I first read *The Daisy Chain*, Erica and I were just starting out, still learning the edges of each other's worlds. I remember thinking, Wow—here's this cool chick who likes to write, and I like to write too... but I wasn't prepared for what I was about to read.

I stayed up until three in the morning, unable to put the book down. Dannah's story gripped me—the grit, the heartbreak, the unrelenting fire in her. I remember finishing the last page and realizing I couldn't wait until morning to tell Erica how incredible it was. I think I called her right then and there, in the dead of night, just to say, "This is amazing."

And I wasn't the only one it captivated. I gave a copy to my mom—who is a voracious reader, one of those people who devours books like air—and she felt the same way. The Daisy Chain wasn't just a Western. It wasn't just a story of survival. It was a force, something raw and impossible to ignore, much like the woman who wrote it.

Because that's the thing about Erica—she's a gale wind that gets under your coat collar and grips you. She's passionate, relentless, and unforgettable—just like Dannah. There is no reading The Daisy Chain without feeling the weight of its words, the dust of its world, the fire of its heroine.

And now, all these years later, re-reading *The Daisy Chain*, I am struck by how it still cuts to the bone, still sings with the kind of storytelling that makes you feel it deep in your ribs. The revised and expanded edition doesn't just bring new depth to the novel—it reminds me why I fell in love with it in the first place.

And if this is your first time reading it, I envy you. Because you're about to experience something unforgettable.

—Erica's Soulmate Dustin

PREFACE

I am Dannah. We all are to an extent. We all take parts of our past, whether tragic or just tragically part of life, and we bury them. Twisting them into a space that fits snugly into our minds, distorting reality into what could only be called our reality.

This story is not a pure work at all; it's one woman's reality. It is this one woman locked in battle with just about every other element: men, nature, self, fate, and society. If the reader can see this story as being told through Dannah Marshall's eyes, then they can also open their perspective to a broader view of these characters.

Dannah is determined as hell and she's got fire in her belly, but she's not whole. She is far too visceral and blinded by past victimizations. Although a young character, she has been molded into her surroundings like the Medea River basin. To some, Cole might appear a happy-go-lucky chap, but he is infected with a don't-act/react response. He is continuously bullied and pushed about in the wind. Henry Edwards, although he is obviously power hungry and narcissistic; he's also vehemently loyal and ambitious. He has been let down by everyone around him. Elizabeth, as a character and a reflection of Dannah, is certainly good-natured and faithful, but she's also fear-filled to the point of being paralyzed. And Billy is rough and tyrannical, but he too suffers from feeling powerless and irrelevant to his world.

My hope is that you will enjoy this history with no such definitions as good or bad. My wish is that the layers of these characters, even the four-legged ones, will unfold to you as they have to me over the years. These peoples, these tendencies live in all of us. More than a century later, all the terrain has been staked, but most of us have yet to settle into ourselves.

AN UPDATE FROM THE AUTHOR
REVISED & EXPANDED EDITION

The first draft of The Daisy Chain was finished in 2007, after years of writing around the edges of my life—scenes scribbled late at night, dialogue pieced together in notebooks, quiet hopes threaded through chaos. When I first published it in 2011, I let it go into the world just as it was —raw, intimate, and entirely mine.

But stories, I've come to learn, don't stay still. They live. They shift. And sometimes, they call you back.

This revised & expanded edition is my return—not to fix what was broken, but to tend to it. To honor what I wrote then, and to bring it forward with everything I've learned since. I've smoothed some seams, deepened some arcs, added new scenes. But the bones remain. The voice remains. Dannah's fire still burns.

Part of what reignited this journey was watching my husband experience his own creative rebirth. This year, he began a journey to complete manuscripts he'd been holding onto for decades. Something about that courage, that claiming of unfinished stories, lit a fuse in me. And I realized: The Daisy Chain isn't finished either. Not really.

Because over the countless edits, re-readings, and nights spent walking its dust-covered roads again, one truth became clear—Cole Edwards has more to say. His story, his reckoning, his need for closure—it demanded to be heard. Whether that ending is redemptive or ruinous, I can't say yet. But I know he deserves it. And so, The Cole Edwards Saga begins.

And still, the prequel to that, this story—Dannah's story—remains the root. She is flint and stubborn will. She is hurt, and hunger and heat. I am Dannah. In more ways than I can count. And maybe, so are you. Because we all bury things. We all twist memory into something we can live with. This book—this fictitious world—isn't about heroes and villains. It's about survival. About the echoes that live in us.

The Daisy Chain is not a clean story. It's a layered one. And if you let it, it will unspool slowly. There are no neat endings here. Only truths buried in dirt and love and legacy.

Thank you for returning. Or arriving. Thank you for walking back into Medea and letting it change you. I hope you see something of yourself in these pages. I hope you're moved. I hope it lingers.

We don't always get to rewrite our stories. But sometimes, we get to add a new chapter.

—Erica M. Goros

THE OFFICIAL PLAYLIST OF THE DAISY CHAIN

Every story has a sound. These are the songs that echo the people and the places—the stolen moments and the notes that linger above the sharpened edges of this journey. Save on Spotify to enjoy the full playlist.

Daisy Chain Official Playlist

A great country for men & dogs, but hell on women
& horses.

— OLD TEXAS PROVERB

CHAPTER ONE

annah breaks into a furious run. Her stomps against the hillside seem to force the damp earth into steep stairs out in front of her, but still, she breathes her way up the escarpment and further away from the river Medea. Heavy boot in front of an even heavier one, and in her memory, Dannah hears a thunderous horse's gallop against the riverbank.

It was nearly a year ago, the longest year of Dannah's life, that Clare, her mama, was tied and dragged behind that fierce horse she can hear in her head. And it was upon the very same stretch of riverbed that she is running on now.

Her mama's pain-filled howls are mere whispers that just float in Dannah's mind, but they circle over and over again hauntingly.

Today, a blanket of thick and strange silence hangs low

inside the tree canopy as it did that day, and it brings her back, all too vividly. She had watched as her mother's body traced graceful wavy lines deep into the muddy bank. It had brought back drawings she made as a girl with her trusty stick on the wet clay shoreline.

She could hear the soft dragging sound that her mother's limp body made against the earth. Dannah had been tied atop the steed, and the *sssh-whoosh* resonated from the ground and filled her ears.

This memory, much like all of Dannah Marshall's past, she only managed to see in brief flashes, but it was still like reliving a horrible ghost story. Dannah had tried to shake the musky smells and the sounds that bounced from bank to bank over the river, but they always came back to her in bits, time and time again.

The river originates as a mere trickle 400 miles northwest of Medea County, Texas, and ends a giant, emptying into the Gulf of Mexico. It came to be a highly traveled route from the Port of Galveston.

Germans, Belgians, Poles, and other immigrants pass through the beating heart of Medea in search of western plots yet to be settled. Ambitious promises of enterprise seem to dangle just in front of the wagon train.

The western region is said to be respite from wild beasts and Injuns. But settlers soon find out they have gone too far. The climate is intolerable, and the terrain is near impossible to work.

They came by steamboat at $300 a fare or from the

north as far as the rail can take them. They forged forward in Conestogas with wheels that reach a grown man's eye. Stretches of land embroidered with sweet flowers but shadowed by great hills were so harsh, a short wagon ride would churn butter.

Pulled by yokes of oxen, they hauled cargo of raisins, dried beef, vinegar, kerosene, and cartridges by the ton. Many women were said to have lost a limb or worse when, without warning, their skirt would catch one of the mammoth wheels, pulling them under, sometimes with a child in hand.

To Dannah Marshall, there could be no sadder sight than seeing a wagon train stopped for a burial. She shivered every time she saw a crucifix in a field. It was odd how it stood out in spite of the tall grass.

They passed the plantations, tenant farms, and windpumps of the east, and ventured into the cattle ranches of the Balcones Escarpment, thankful for the occasional message scrawled upon a rock that heeded warnings like Do not drink water.

Tired in spirit and depleted in numbers, whether from an accident, altercation, or any of the diseases that would strike at will — cholera, consumption, diphtheria, or typhoid.

Medeans often tried to warn passersby not to venture too much further. But something kept them moving toward what lay beyond the next crest. Dannah thought perhaps they weren't as foolish as they were painted. The town of Medea, after all, had its scoundrels. At least the immigrants had each other.

Dannah's Mama used to say the heart of a person only beats when it's surrounded by blood, by family. But Mama's blood had since been leached and drained in her recovery. Dannah did not quite understand what kept her breathing after the dragging. It seemed to her something much darker red than blood had kept her alive.

To Dannah and her sister Elisabeth, something strange had happened. In a way, the dragging had actually woke Mama up. She didn't speak much and never got out of bed, but her eyes were more alive now. Only the girls could see it.

The Doc and another townsman had carried Mama back to the cabin. She was naked spare a few strips of cloth that the rocks hadn't grated off of her. Her first moments of consciousness were spent staring at Dannah through a swollen and bloodied eye. Her mouth remained slightly agape, showcasing the deep holes where teeth were once planted.

"She looks like a little baby, Dan, just like a baby." Elisabeth marveled. Dannah didn't marvel.

Her ma whispered, "Hannah, I'm sorry."

Mama was the only one who still used her given name. "Hannah, I've ruined you." She said ever-so-faintly and fell back out of consciousness.

Mama used to tell vivid stories of her transformation from Hannah to Dannah. Said by the time she was five, she had made up her mind; she wanted to be like her pa.

Ma said Dannah would sob if she wasn't allowed to go into the field with Pa. "Had absolutely no use for staying in the cabin with her own mama and sister." And that one time, she pitched a fit so bad after Pa left without her, she turned blue. "You almost washed away the cabin with your tears," Mama would tell her, "like the river in springtime."

Dannah did remember putting on her father's boots. They came clean up to her rear end, and she would stomp around the cabin as loud as she could muster. Since she could recall, she had come to be called Dannah, after her father, Daniel John Marshall.

Her ma always said she loved her spirit, just as she did Daniel's, but "Hannah, you remember, you're a girl and someday a woman." It just wasn't right, a lady in a man's boots or wearing a man's name. Mama came to tolerate it.

She had been Hannah once—soft and small. A name that fit neatly inside a mother's mouth, but she had outgrown it. Dannah was sharper, more grounded. It carried her father's name, his boots, his world. And she had taken it on because she had needed to. Because a Hannah would not have survived here.

After the dragging, Elisabeth wanted to ask Mama if she thought a horse always had a quarter on the ground or if it got all four legs up when it ran, like it was soaring. She read an article in *The Democratic Statesman* that her grandfather had sent down from Austin about a bet between two men of science. The paper detailed an

Eadweard Muybridge and his $25,000 bet about a race-horse's stride.

Elisabeth retold the details of the electric trigger he used to set off his many cameras. The series of pictures proved that the animal does indeed get all fours off the ground at once. Subsequent articles sent by their grandfather told of Muybridge's later infamy at his murder trial.

Apparently, upon discovering his wife's infidelities, he paid a visit to one Major Harry Larkyns, said "Good Evening, Major, my name is Muybridge and here is the answer to the letter you sent my wife," thereupon he shot him dead. He was freed by reason of justifiable homicide.

Elisabeth was always reading, reciting, and coming up with questions no one could answer. Dannah never would allow her sister to ask Ma if horses fly. It probably would have tickled Mama though. She adored Elisabeth's curiosity; Dannah loathed it.

They were on their own now. There should be no time for such fanciful thinking. Besides, it didn't seem fair to ask if, in-between a lashing, half-drowning, and a drag-ging, she had looked up to study her persecutors — Sheriff Hillard and his horse.

Elisabeth had a theory that the river had actually protected her. "Mama didn't feel any of those rocks, roots, or rope. I think the only thing she did feel was the Almighty knocking some sense into her."

But that was Lizzie, older in years, but not in life. When she was around fifteen years old, she caught the fever. Doctors said it weakened her heart. She never really left the ranch after that. She even made Dannah sell her preserves and pick up the mending work at the neighbors'. Since their father Daniel left the family, Dannah took care of all the ranching. Elisabeth took care of Mama and some of the housework. And Mama, well now, Mama just slept.

CHAPTER TWO

$\mathcal{D}$annah came back to the here and now, and she shook off thoughts of the past. She made her way across the field, managing to outrun the wind-charged grass. She didn't slow down as she jumped on the hay pile. She learned years ago to run upon it like she would mount a steed. Her heart seemed to be beating louder than her gasps for air.

Straddled atop the monstrous pile, she watched as the sky opened up for the first time today, just in time to reveal the sun starting its surrender. Piercing bits of cobalt light emerged from behind the sunken grey clouds. With the sun squeezing through the heavy-handed charcoal streaks, it looked to her like an open mouth ready to gobble her up.

She tilted her round face up towards the sky and closed her eyes as if inhaling the clouds and the little blazes of heavens through her nose. Her auburn-brown strands undulated back and forth in the wind like she was underwater.

She threw back her arms with force, as if she hoped to ride the current, and clenched her thighs down on the hay for flight. But the only thing to soar would be a bellow that rose from deep within her belly.

She didn't intend to yell, but her throat gave way without warning her first. It startled her eyes open and reminded her of the work yet unfinished. Dannah hurried back to the cabin to finish up her woodpile before worrying about supper. She burst into the cabin to look for her ax, but her sister Elisabeth stopped her with a high-toned plea.

"Will you forget about chopping the wood, just for today, and come help me with the preserves? Like we used to!" Elisabeth's gaze begged from across the kitchen.

Elisabeth's eyes always had a way of cutting right through Dannah's undaunted demeanor. They were shaped like two spades lying on their sides, almost tip-to-tip, and they had a way of picking up every hint of light in a room, the way a prism does.

"Dearest sister, without wood to burn, how do you suppose we bring up the preserves? We would've had enough for the week, if not for that damn Edwards boy." Dannah stripped off her boot and began to adjust the tattered bandages that wound around each toe.

"Dannah, Billy's father would have his hide if he found

out Billy had set one hair of his head near our cabin. Besides, he's just being a boy … with better things to do than chop wood, like splashin' around Hamilton Pond like we used to do. We'll stop him next time, I'm sure of it." Elisabeth tied back her fair hair and poured a large dose of molasses and ginger into the pot on the cookstove.

Dannah tugged her boot back over her poorly wrapped foot. "Better hope you catch him, not me." She was more agitated by her sister's vigorous defense of an Edwards boy than her ill-fitting boot.

"Oh, hush, and fetch me that spoon," Elisabeth said, grabbing a handful of carrots and a couple dried oranges from inside a cheesecloth. Dannah watched her dump the slices into boiling water, thinking back to the time when they used to be able to use sugar instead of molasses and fresh lemons, not vinegar.

"Well, Elisabeth," she barked back suddenly, "it's not like I am going to go knock on that Billy's door, and he damn well knows it." Dannah knew if she were to venture over to the Edward's ranch ever again, she'd be gunning after Henry Edwards, Billy's father.

"Don't matter. Me and Queeny'll catch him, right girl?" Dannah's mouth melted into a grin as she rubbed the underside of the dog's ears and entertained thoughts of catching Billy in the act of stealing from her.

Queeny was a droopy-eyed, droopy-eared, all-around mess of a mutt that her pa had brought home from the Wilkinson's orchard as a pup. Ma had named her Queen

Esther on account of her noble disposition. But she looked like a haggard thing even as a pup.

She was supposed to be a field hound, and Pa had high hopes for a trusted companion. But ol' Queeny slept late, snored, was deaf in one ear from the litter, and limped from a run in with a wild goose as a pup. It didn't take too long for Pa to give up on Queeny altogether.

Ma secretly confessed that Queeny had won, she had Pa beat. She told the girls that one day they could take a lesson from Queen Esther. When they were all grown and understood the dealings of men and women, they'd have a great laugh at her triumph over the master.

Ma would jostle Queeny's ears back and forth in satisfaction and then drop a tiny morsel of stew meat near her highness. She'd always pretend not to have noticed dropping it though. Maybe it was her guilt over wasting good salt-cured meat or the fact that Pa would have kicked that dog out for the coyotes, if he had known. But Queeny made sure to lick all the evidence away, and Ma made sure Pa's plate was amply full.

That was the way she was back then, always happy to be alive and so tenderhearted. Dannah had even seen Mama fake ill for a week when food was running really short, so Pa and the girls could have their fill. Queeny would go without then, too.

Dannah didn't put it together at the time, but when Pa'd go off in the morning, she had often seen her ma chewing on birch bark and filling a cup with kerosene-

canned fruit that had turned bad. She was believable too; lack of food and bad vittles made her pale and sickly looking on more than one occasion.

When Dannah was old enough and had proven herself with a gun, her mother turned her loose on all the large vermin to be had. Of course, Ma figured she was simply keeping her occupied and out of trouble, until one day she came back with a turkey. After that day, she put Dannah on hunting duty more often.

That damn gobbler had put up quite the fight though. Dannah had no idea how fast they could run. The river bird came straight at her and Cole Edwards, her hunting companion. The loose skin that framed its beak and skinny neck turned scarlet red before it made its charge. After the attack, Dannah and Cole concurred it must have been a stray from a farm because wild turkeys run from their own shadow.

At first, Ma made Elisabeth accompany Dannah on her hunt, on account of her being older. That is until she realized Elisabeth still had a chance of being a lady, and by then Dannah was hopeless.

Dannah took up arms regularly with their neighbor to the east and the older of the Edwards boys, Cole. Together they prowled for possum, squirrel, anything big enough to eat, really. Cole was four years older than her and had always been a foot taller, but she could out-shoot, out-run, and out-wrangle him any day of the week and twice on Sunday. He'd never admit it though; he was always trying to teach her things that she already knew from her days in the fields with Pa.

"Oh, I understand. Thank you, Cole." She'd always say. She was still able to rein in her sarcasm back then.

Dannah often thought of the time they had picked up animal tracks while they were making their way home from an unsuccessful afternoon of fishing. Cole had snatched a fountain darter that he swore up and down must be a "big ol' bass" as he pulled up his pole and presented the tiniest little fish Dannah had ever seen.

Needless to say, the fishing excursion was considered a failure. Cole's mood had soured, and Dannah was finding it hard to enjoy her normally serene afternoon. She felt annoyed by the waste of the beautiful weather, but she had always tried to humor him when his pride got the best of him.

Cole tried to regain himself as he leaned over the tracks they had stumbled upon. "That's a fresh set." He pointed out the series of five-pointed claw marks to her. It always tickled her to watch the way he froze in excitement, like he was intensely listening to them speak.

"Um, Cole, right there … that's a skunk's prints." She warned him, following behind at a safe distance.

"For crying out loud, Dannah, it's a badger. Look at the claws." Cole dismissed her and concentrated on walking gently heel first, avoiding any twigs.

Dannah knelt down and eyeballed the prints closer. The pad was too wide and rounded out to be a badger; she was sure. She smirked in certainty, but she shook off the thoughts of self-satisfaction and ran to stop Cole.

She found him crouched, back against a tree, with the barrel of his gun aimed at a bush. With one hand raised in the air, he stopped her from running right over him.

She slowly came down beside him, level with the bush. "Cole Edwards, I have to go home," Dannah demanded.

He shot her a wicked glance and turned quickly back to the bush. "Quiet, I can hear him." He pushed the words out the corner of his closed mouth.

"But ..." Dannah stopped when she heard rustling. She knew it was too late. She tried to dive onto the ground. But she landed on Cole's calf, which was behind him as he knelt. This threw him forward and further into the skunk's spray.

Not a word was uttered between them on the way back to the cabin. In fact, the only sounds were Dannah's occasional exasperated grunts and the grinding of Cole's jaw.

Dannah let him continue to do the teaching because she felt sorry for him. His pa, Henry Edwards, rode him real hard, and he got licked a lot.

Cole didn't deserve it though; he did everything his father asked. He was not like his younger brother. Billy was Dannah's age, and Cole was just a year older than Elisabeth.

When Dannah was in school, she took ten lashings when Billy snuck playing cards into her desk. Miss Chapman found them when she was tidying up the classroom during recess. She saw the jack of spades peeking out of Dannah's Bible, stuck right to John 7:38: *He that believeth on me, as the scripture hath said, out of his belly shall flow rivers of living water.*

Billy was and always would be trouble. Pulling the girls' braids and stealing the boys' apples and everyone knew it. Everyone except Mr. Henry Edwards, that is.

Henry Edwards downright ran the town of Medea. He wasn't law, but he didn't need a badge to pull the strings of the townspeople. He came to Texas from New York, by way of Kansas in between. He moved here with a land title in one hand, like a thoroughbred, and an invitation from the Republican government stashed away under his hat. He wielded his power through threats.

He had lived here long enough that people forgot he was really a Yankee, but he kept his business ties wound tight enough that people remembered he was quite connected. His family came from the meatpacking industry. Despite rumors of a rift between his brothers, he'd never told anyone why he left, spare some talk of greater stakes to be had.

As more and more settlers came to Medea, he came to be relied upon. He took up with the Sheriff's office an unofficial liaison role. He took what he wanted and got paid through the nose for his so-called protection against desperados and settlers' disputes. Dannah had long since heard if one failed to meet his fee, they'd nearly always get a visit from a rustler in the middle of the night.

No one could afford not to fork over the

"Edwards' tax". And no one ever got a clean count on his herd, but they continued to multiply, and so did his stack of deeds. He made a real nice habit out of making loans and carrying mortgages for folks caught in a hard spot. Of course, he had the biggest ranch in Medea: he had the most hands, the most livestock, and he was the first to put up a barbed fence.

Edwards' wife, Mattie, was quite a bit younger than him and quite the treasure. He brought her back from one of his annual visits to New York like a souvenir. Her family's roots were in lumber mills, although it wasn't apparent. She could hardly be considered hardy stock, but she was dreadfully pretty. Dannah believed Mattie Edwards was the only woman in Medea to have never held a hoe or handled a herd on her own. Yet she spotted something in the way Mattie held herself that gave her away as used. She could never put her finger on what it was, though. Perhaps it was just city living; city women were a different breed.

She had a dainty, slender build and big brown doe eyes that sloped downward under a long black line of lashes. She wore rouge and perfume and always left the neckline unbuttoned on her fancy dresses, showing off her creamy white complexion. It was hard to tell if the women in town were more distraught over her boldness or her swanky clothes.

When Dannah was younger, she couldn't understand how Mattie didn't notice them mocking her. Now she realized that she was playing the gallery, and she loved the attention. A real cultured lady among peasants, or conversely, to the women of Medea, a whore among good Christians.

Medea fancied itself God-fearing. Church was in the schoolhouse every Sunday along with spelling bees, sewing circles, and basket picnics each summer. The schoolhouse had just finished being rebuilt after an unfortunate lightning strike last spring.

Dannah only made it through third grade. Most boys didn't last that long, and she was one of the last girls still in class. A few made it to fifth, but for Dannah, third was a blessing.

Elisabeth went to school for little while too, but one day she just up and started crying every morning. So after a while, Ma caved and let her stay home.

"Guess you've outlearned your teacher, anyways." She reasoned at the overwrought girl.

Ma said she got her brains from Grandpa. He was a teacher, a real university professor. The girls had only met their Grandfather John twice, maybe a third time when they were younger. He had been living in Austin for a few years and now taught at the new University of Texas.

Elisabeth could read circles around their teacher, Miss Chapman, and everyone Dannah knew, except their Ma.

Ma said Lizzie was just scared of people. "Our Elisabeth is as timid as a hummingbird. She's just scared of what people have the ability to hide in plain sight."

So she never really got used to other people, and after

she fell ill, Elisabeth hardly met anyone she didn't read about or dream up.

The last week of every month, most months anyway, Pa used to make a special trip into town to fetch her a new book. First thing he'd do, before he even left Mr. Stone's Bookstore, was write "The property of Miss Elisabeth Anne Marshall" with the date on the inside cover.

After their pa left home, she pleaded for Dannah to go to Stone's for her, and Dannah occasionally did. She'd reluctantly stroll into the store; Mr. Stone would look up from his typesetting with a familiar nod. Then he would leave the room, returning a few minutes later with a new book he'd swear she hadn't read. "This is the one! This one has giants in it." But even Mr. Hollinger Stone had trouble keeping track.

Elisabeth usually paid for books with mending money she'd earned from a couple of the neighboring bachelors and from selling some of her red chokeberry preserve to the ranch hands. Eventually, it became a regular old library in the cabin. Dannah let the tradition of inscribing her sister's books die with her father's absence.

Mr. Stone should have thanked the Marshalls. Elisabeth was one of his only loyal customers, even if most of them were dime novels and chap books. She did occasionally splurge; she bought that Tom Sawyer book just last Christmas for Elisabeth. Medea was actually very lucky to have a little bookstore.

Most townspeople had read the same Sears-Roebuck catalogue hanging on their privy walls for years. If it weren't for a handful of other transplanted literates, Mr. Stone would have had to survive on their jam money alone.

Stone and the rest of the store owners in town were walking a little lighter these days, with scuttlebutt of the rail workers coming through. It meant more mending and washing work to be had, and Dannah would be grateful for that.

CHAPTER THREE

*D*annah got through her wood chopping fairly quickly, and the girls settled in for an earlier supper than usual. Elisabeth nibbled on a minuscule portion of cornmeal mush and had already found her favorite reading spot near the hearth. "Lizzie, what are you reading?" Dannah asked from across the cabin.

The cabin was small but sturdy, its log walls darkened by years of smoke and weather. A low-beamed ceiling held the warmth close, and the hearth, always burning or smoldering, cast flickering light across the packed-earth floor. Rough-hewn shelves sagged under the weight of tin dishes, dried herbs, and their precious books. Near the fire, an old rocking chair sat angled just so, with a wool blanket draped over the back. The table in the center was scratched and uneven, but it held their bowls and bread like any fine dining room might. A single narrow window looked out toward the kitchen garden; the latch worn smooth by Dannah's hands. Everything inside bore the mark of usefulness first, comfort second—but still, the place held warmth, especially when the girls were laughing.

Dannah had left her second bowl of cornmeal on the table and kept returning for heaping mouthfuls in between tidying up the cabin. "I'm rereading *The Geography and Tribes of Western Africa* by Lord William Thornton," answered Lizzie.

She flipped the page, not paying Dannah too much mind. "I would like to see Africa one day," Elisabeth said almost to herself.

"Then we will have to go." Dannah peeked over at her in the chair by the fire. "I heard the animals there have a taste for people, though."

Dannah's voice got deeper and slower as she continued, "Elephants that swallow you whole..." She let her voice fall back to a normal tone

"When shall we go?"

Elisabeth exclaimed, "Oh, you are evil! Elephants don't eat people. They are quite dangerous, though, because of their immense size," she said, turning back to an illustration.

"Dannah," she closed the book, folded her legs up, and leaned forward in her seat. "I saw them today," her voice a shade quieter. "Sheriff Hillard. Henry Edwards. They were standing near the kitchen garden. They didn't come up to the cabin. What did you think they wanted?"

Dannah could feel her cheeks rush suddenly with

warmth, but she deliberately forced her brow and her voice downward. "You just watch the wood supply, and you let Queeny loose if you see them again." She rushed the words out and abruptly turned for bed.

Elisabeth called after her, "Henry Edwards would rather eat wood, than take ours. Why do you really think they were here?"

She entered calmly back into the kitchen and tugged on her shirt. "Yes, well, he has no problem with our cattle and our land. You don't think he would lower himself for our wood?" Dannah bit her lip. She did not like to involve Lizzie in business matters; it always upset her too much.

"Well, maybe we can give Queen Esther here a taste for human blood, like those elephants of yours?" Dannah gave one of Queeny's jutting ears a stiff tug too, then came back to her bowl, shoveling the last heap into her mouth.

"I'm going to bed," she said with food still in the back of her throat. She left Elisabeth alone with Queeny and her elephants.

CHAPTER FOUR

On certain days when the sun rose just right over the river, Dannah too felt God-fearing. By the time the river reached Medea, it opened up to a great surge, carving out rock and land in its path. Dannah knew it was the blood that had flown on its banks that made it pound so hard inside Medea.

Must have been trying to escape, she thought as she fished in the early light. It mustered all of its strength to run to the other side of Medea as fast as it could, like she raced the wind in the fields. It was as if the river were being hunted by spear-carrying natives from Elisabeth's Africa books. The water out-swiped its predator with every curve and twist.

Dannah stared through her warped reflection and into the water's depths. She realized the cradle of the river was deep and thick, same as it ever was. Her path was not changed by men, but by time alone. She was engraved upon the earth. That's why sometimes she's fickle and overflows and sometimes she's hauntingly tranquil and dries up.

The land around Medea breathed with a quiet, rugged beauty—a place where limestone outcrops shouldered up through the soil like old bones, and gnarled live oaks cast their shadows across hills that rolled like gentle swells. The Medea River, clear and cold as poured glass, traced a serpentine course through the valley, flanked by cypress trees with roots knuckled deep into the earth. Their pale green canopies shimmered in the wind like the fringe of a faded curtain.

Here, the earth bore the scent of cedar smoke and wild sage, and in the spring, bluebonnets bloomed like indigo spilled ink across the hillsides, painting the rough terrain with soft defiance. Life was hard bitten, carved from rock and dust, but the land sang with a strange, enduring grace —a place of mule trails and dry creek beds, of cardinals flashing red against the grey-green brush.

Farther east and south, the Hill Country unfurled in wide, sun-bleached expanses that led toward San Antonio de Béxar, a city still shaking off the weight of old Spain and the shadow of the Republic. The city stood as a crossroads between the wild and the civilized, its adobe walls and limestone missions weathered by time, its plazas echoing with Spanish, German, and the steady rhythm of Tejano boots.

The terrain beyond was a land of contrasts: high ridges crumbling into canyons, mesquite and cactus thriving in the same breath as peach orchards and grazing cattle. Water was gold, and those who claimed it—via spring, well, or river—held the key to survival. Comanche trails still haunted the edges of recent memories, and settlers, many of them newly arrived immigrants, watched the horizon with wary hope.

To the untrained eye, it was a land of thorns and stone. But to those who lived it—who sweated in its fields, prayed in its chapels, and buried their dead in its stony soil—it was a land that remembered. A land that required grit. A land that repaid faith with beauty and silence with sudden song.

Dannah gave up on fishing with no luck on her line. The post office would be opening soon, and she was eager for good news about the land inquiry.

The town was not as sleepy as some would suppose, a bustling burrow to pass through from the southern corridor on the way to the Chisholm Trail. It acted as a budding trading outpost, with the last Indian-inhabited territory to the north. And just to the west, a fruitless country of splintered ground and patches of thirsty grass not worthy of feeding goats.

In fact, Medea boasted the last stretch of good farming soil clean into Mexico. The river lay just on the outskirts, and the town itself was built on a basin, a flat molded-out shape that formed a perfect horseshoe just around the jailhouse. Dannah always thought that it was fitting; Sheriff Hillard liked to keep his eyes on the town and his fingers within reach of their purses.

He hadn't bothered the Marshalls since the dragging. Maybe the old bastard felt guilty, but Dannah knew it wouldn't last forever. Sheriff Hillard and Henry Edwards' visit to the ranch made her certain of that.

Their consciences must have been clearing, at least the Sheriff's was. Edwards didn't have one and would never leave them alone. He had no blood coursing through his veins. He simply lived off theirs.

The Post Office sat snugly between Walter's General Store and The Grand Bank of Central Texas. Dannah tore open the bleached Pony Express envelope clearly marked from the Land Commissioner's as if there could be nothing but redemption inside.

She had done everything by the book, even made an official plea to the state for her title. They were practically paying people to take over the western acres to fund the rail. They couldn't deny her own land, the land she'd worked since she was a child.

"There's the face that launched a thousand ships!" A voice boomed.

Dannah didn't have to look up to see who was speaking. He leaned his hand against the wall over her head. His hat smashed inside his grasp, and in the other hand, he held the book *Greek Heroes*. Dannah had read that title from Elisabeth's collection at least three or four times.

He lowered his head and chest within inches of her face using the wall for leverage, tilting toward her as if he were asking for the next waltz. He let go of a big smug grin.

It was Cole Edwards.

"Edwards, I'm afraid you have the wrong character," she said matter-of-factly, tapping on his book. She then rather exaggeratedly folded her letter back into its envelope and tucked it into the waistband of her skirt.

"What—you are not so innocent, huh?" He smirked, not letting up his intense gaze for a moment.

"Oh, but I am innocent. And you are without any golden apples to toss in my path, so kindly move out of my way." Dannah stood very still, as if she were waiting for her schoolmistress Miss Chapman's ruler to come down upon her arm. But really, she was waiting for her own composure to be restored. If it was a battle of wits he wanted, nights of Elisabeth reading aloud had her armed, and she would win. She always did.

"I shall use my body to stop you from blazing." He inched his chin even closer, so she could not look away or even move her head.

Dannah, still determined to outwit him, brought her focus down from the doorway behind him and into the very center of his irises.

She squinted at his pupils as if to shoot the words directly into him like an archer. "Then I shall have to use my knife to stop your body." And with that, she twisted out from under his arm, only to hear him yell rather wryly after her.

"If only your blade were as sharp as your tongue, you'd have sliced me through years ago."

She couldn't help herself; her composure was done for.

He had won. She tore off a land advertisement that hung in the entrance, crumbled it into a ball and lashed it backward at Cole's face. "Tell your father to stay off my land, or he will be able to tell you exactly what my knife feels like."

"What was that fuss about?" Cole asked her fleeing shadow in the doorway. Dannah slipped around to the side of the Post Office to finish reading the letter and overheard the Postmaster, the gossipy fool he was, answering Cole's question.

"She's been getting letters concerning her land situation. They are coming 'round once a month."

"He's got no right," Dannah grumbled aloud as she thought much more violent words of Postmaster Roberson. "No better than that quilting-bee wife of his, running his bazoo all over town."

Cole had tried everything to spark some recollection in Dannah. To get her to admit what they once were to each other.

They had always been the best of friends, hunting buddies, but they had grown to be much more than that. She had stirred a part of him that he didn't realize existed until Dannah had found it.

She had awakened it from deep within, but set him calm everywhere else, and he knew he had softened the rough edges that life had carved on her. Now, he felt holes open up in his stomach every time he remembered that they were no longer ... they were no longer anything.

Dannah watched Cole run across the street on his

heels. He unfurled his mashed hat as he entered The Grand Hotel. Henry Edwards had kept a room for his wife, Mattie, at The Grand, since after the first winter they were married. She just wasn't cut out for ranch living. They told people it was to be near the pharmacies and healers in town. Before Doc Olsen moved to town, the nearest real doctor was in Castroville, nearly a half day away by stage.

There were a number of rumors of a congenital heart disorder and of a miscarriage. Dannah didn't really remember them all. Since she could remember, there had been constant chatter after Mattie Edwards left her ranch.

Dannah came out of hiding and picked up the land advertisement that the wind had carried outside the door. She smoothed it across her thigh to read it:

Come along, come along, don't be alarmed; Uncle Sam is rich enough to give us all a farm! Make Your Claim! 160 acres guaranteed, free from Indians, less humid acres to any man who wants it and lives on the land. Yours only $.25 an acre...

She stopped reading when she spotted Henry Edwards out of the corner of her eye, turning into The Grand. She circled back around and into the saloon, convincing herself it was a mad thirst, not a quick madness that brought her inside to bend an elbow at such an early hour.

CHAPTER FIVE

"Pa, why does Dannah Marshall think you've been on her land?" Cole asked, lowering his gaze and smoothing the rim of his hat again and again.

"Not hers." Henry made no attempt to look up at his son. He continued sorting through the mail that Cole had set on the table.

"What do you mean?" Cole asked loud enough that he thought to close the door to his mother's bedroom.

"Belongs to the state," Henry sat down upon the sofa, "that's prime riverfront acreage. The Democrats want more farms down here."

"But I just saw an acre is at $.25?" Cole said, recalling the advertisement from the Post Office.

"Not watered land, son. That's the dried-up shit land to the west that they can't settle anyhow. The railroad big bugs are selling cheap to ease the debt and expand the range of track they can lay."

Henry poured whiskey from a cut-crystal decanter. Dust had settled so heavily in its glass grooves that it appeared to be frosted.

"After I collect on the acres owed to me, that Marshall plot will be too small to sell off. Just good for expanding our ranch and that's just what we are going to do. By hook or crook, the Marshalls ain't keeping that land, son."

"But Dannah knows ranch ways better than I do. Hell, she brought the herd in with her pa every year since she was 11. Single-handedly built that new barn and ..."

"Get out between hay and grass, son," he interrupted. "You can hire her as a hand when we take it over. She should be cheap as a John Chinamen soon enough."

"But the Marshalls owned that land over fifteen years. Only takes five to make them outright owners."

"It's not their land if they can't prove it. They have no deed in their hand. And that's Daniel Marshall's title, not Dannah." Henry gave all of his attention to Cole now and put his letters down. "Daniel Marshall's dead, and that girl's got nothing but his last name. Besides—who's to say their kin didn't side with the Rebs? There are laws for probate issues, and laws are written by the men who use 'em, son. And I intend to use 'em well. Now, pull in your horns."

Most of the saloon patrons had stopped taking notice of Dannah some time ago. They used to freeze up when she started frequenting, weren't used to seeing a non-working girl inside the saloon walls.

But most of the men kept away from her and went about their drinking and carousing, fairly certain she wouldn't be telling anyone's wife about an afternoon visit to the saloon.

"Can I buy you a drink, Miss Dannah?" Clyde Davis seemed particularly bold from his early bender with the whiskey. Must have forgotten they had been through this dance several times before, Dannah thought.

"You're still a lady, fine as cream gravy, even though you got dirty nails and all. But underneath those clothes," Clyde took his finger and twirled up a piece of her hair that had fallen from out of her hat, "I'm sure you're a real fine lady, cursed or not."

Now this was a mistake, the stupid mudsill. "Hum, you know, you're right, Clyde." Dannah turned toward him and let her chin rest upon his pinched fingers.

Surprised, he released the sprig of hair. "I could use a drink," she said as coyly as she could muster without making herself nauseous. Dannah's ink-filled eyes buzzed about for a moment and then steadied on Clyde.

"I knew it, I knew there was something between us Dannah. I seen it in the way you looks at me. I tried to tell old Joe." He whistled his S's through tiny foul and blackened teeth and winked at his lunger friend, Joseph, at the table in front.

And he was right; there was something between them. Five coins her hand found in his filthy jacket pocket. She took down the drink straight away and pried his sweaty little fingers away from her. They had somehow made their way back to that stray piece of hair.

"Let me get this one Clyde, you buy next time." She threw two of his coins down on the bar and pocketed the others, grabbed her hat and headed for the fields. She was already behind for the day.

That night after enjoying two helpings of supper, Dannah undressed early. The rains had brought out a mess of mosquitoes, which had feasted on her all afternoon. Her ranch hands did not seem too bothered by them, though. It must have been the sugarcane in her system that had attracted them. She had bought it as a treat for Lizzie and Ma.

She gathered up some chickweed on the way home and mixed it with vinegar to bathe with. She soaked herself with a towel as she settled into bed. It brought the swelling down enough for her to lie still a few minutes at a time without scratching.

Suddenly Queeny started yelping like she was having one of her goose dreams, but Dannah found her wide-awake, pacing at the doorway.

Dannah threw on her boots and grabbed the shotgun from the corner of the kitchen. "You think it's a cayot trying to get into the chicken coop again?" Elisabeth said still tucked up into her usual ball, reading near the fire.

"Could be. Or maybe, it's Billy trying to make off with our hens." Dannah pulled her nightgown down over her head. As soon as the door opened, Queeny dashed about 300 feet ahead of her, howling like a banshee. She ran toward what Dannah could only make out as a black mass on the ground.

She spotted the heap in her sights as she walked closer, favoring her right side in long, deliberate strides. She stopped five feet shy of the mound on the ground and cocked her rifle. The moon shone just enough through the clouds to reveal Cole Edwards' face with a hell of a swollen black eye.

She hovered over him, listening intently. It was as though he was trying to say something, and she leaned closer only to realize he was singing. The stupid boy was roostered.

Elisabeth came up behind Dannah with a candle to light her way. "What's wrong with him?" Elisabeth asked, nearly getting knocked down by Queeny's bouncing. The old girl was looking for praise on being such a good half-deaf scout.

"Probably got into a brawl at the saloon."

Elisabeth leaned in, too, to see his swollen face and started to laugh. "Looks like he lost." Queeny continued to jump all over Elisabeth with growing excitement, nearly knocking her onto the ground next to Cole.

"Smells like he didn't feel it much." Dannah said, not able to help but echo her sister's chuckles. "Let's go to bed." Dannah turned to leave, now as pleased as Queeny.

"We can't just leave him here." Elisabeth stood her ground. Neither of them was laughing now.

"The hell I can't. He's on my property; I don't owe him anything."

"Dannah, please. For me?" She paused for a response. "At least, let's put him in the barn," Elisabeth bargained.

"Sister, you are asking me to invite the devil in for dinner."

"He's not the devil and you know it!"

Dannah peered down at Cole again with disgust. "For you, sister," she grunted at Elisabeth and crouched down to pick up his arms, "Well … grab his legs."

Elisabeth followed the instructions, and even Queen

Esther jumped in to help. She wedged herself between the girls and proceeded to clamp down on his right thigh, then began making jerking pulls as she pranced backwards, helping. It took them a good ten minutes to get him to the chicken coop, which they settled on since it was closer than the barn.

When they finally made it inside, Dannah let go of the lock she had around his arms. His head was the first thing to hit the ground with a loud *donk*. Elisabeth was forced to follow when Cole's weight almost pulled her to the ground too. But Queen Esther held tight to Cole's thigh.

Dannah could almost see Queeny's grin through Cole's trousers, as his leg hung suspended about two feet off the ground, as limp as a marionette. She chuckled at her proud beast.

"Go inside before it starts to rain and take Queeny with you before she remembers how old she is." Dannah ordered.

Elisabeth tapped Queeny square atop her head with her pointer finger, and she released her grip on Cole's thigh, perched her ears back, and followed her out of the coop with a spry bounce.

Dannah followed behind them, but couldn't close up the coop, because Cole's feet didn't quite clear the doorway. She let out an annoyed groan and gave his boot a fierce kick, sending the chickens into a clucking frenzy. She straddled over his calves and bent each limp leg up, one by one.

All at once, Cole jolted straight up and grabbed her with the *thwap* of his open palm against the nape of her neck and pulled her down to his eye level. When the slap came down, the force nearly sent her headfirst into his chest. He was supporting all of his weight with her neck.

"I defended yous," he said with a slur. "He, he said you were a thief," Cole fell back against the ground, and Dannah collapsed backward between his legs. "Fifteen coins … I don't believe it. Not my Dannah, no" he mumbled before he closed his eyes again.

She stood up, brushing the hay off her nightgown, cricking her neck from side to side, and peered down at him. "I ain't yours, crowbait." She gave his ankle a good kick. "And it was five."

It was starting to rain as she walked back to the cabin. She felt every muscle in her neck flame up as she drug a wooden trunk behind the door.

Dannah lay in bed listening to the sheets of rain that were hitting the cabin get harder and harder. She felt a few droplets on her arm and made a mental note to fetch some sand and chink the gaps that the storms had opened up. She rolled over and fell half asleep quickly, but her mind soon turned to the falls that summer and the water beating down on her from above.

She used to love to sneak off to them, her private paradise or so she reckoned. But Billy Edwards, the little pervert, had discovered her haven, and he made off with her clothes one particularly humid day. If it hadn't been for Cole, she would have had to cover herself in switch-grass like some inbred out of one of Elisabeth's books.

She didn't even know about the theft until Cole

announced himself abruptly with a shotgun to his brother's back. They stood above Dannah, high atop the flattened-out rock that narrowly bridged the falls above.

Dannah stopped flailing about on the surface when she heard them. "Billy has something to tell you, Dannah." She looked up at two sun-silhouetted figures she knew could only be the Edwards boys.

"Here." Billy dropped a rumpled pile of clothes. She recognized her faded blue skirt on top. The boys were turned sideways toward the woods to the east, so not to face her in the water. Cole gave a swift kick to his brother, striking him behind the left knee.

Billy buckled. "Sorry!" He hadn't quite gotten the word out before he swiveled up to his feet and went in to punch Cole in the chest. Cole was ready for it though; he leaned back out of range of the swing. Billy settled for spitting at his face before he scrambled off into the woods.

"I am sorry." He cleared his throat loudly. "About Billy, he likes to stir things up. He didn't mean no harm."

"And what exactly are you doing here? Watching him, watch me?"

Flustered at Dannah's reaction, Cole replied, "Well, I wouldn't have thought you so bold, for such a little girl. You have to be more careful round here and more modest."

She ignored him. "I spotted some new tracks outside the north line of oaks, figured we could do some exploring this week?"

"Dannah, I don't have time to play, I have work to do.

I'll leave the baby games to you." He said, using the barrel of his gun to trace a series of lines in the dirt around his feet.

"I'm not a baby!" She howled up at him with such force that Cole looked straight at her in the water. It took him a moment to realize he was staring straight at Dannah naked.

He hadn't meant to look. God knew he hadn't meant to see. No matter how many times he blinked, her image stuck like a sunspot behind his eyes.

He'd always known her as a wild thing, half-boy in manner, full of splinters and sharp edges—but there in the water, all that noise went quiet. Her hair was lit with streaks of auburn when the sun hit just right. She was strong, built like the land—sun-fed but soft at all the curves. She looked like something that couldn't be owned, only witnessed. And maybe that's what gutted him most— he'd thought of her as a chum with dirt under her nails and no time for dreams and a hell of a good trouble- seeking compadre. But now, in that instant, he knew better. With this flash of seeing her undone, he unraveled.

Cole caught his breath in his chest, kicked the ground clean of the little lines and watched the gravel hurl piece by piece over the edge. Then Cole ran off into the woods too.

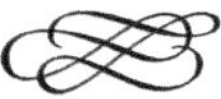

CHAPTER SEVEN

*D*annah made her way to the herd in the morning, and Cole was still fast asleep in the coop. She was glad of it, too. There was a long day ahead with no more time for his flannel-mouthed lies. She had to make sure none of the steers had gone and drowned themselves.

Cole awoke to the sounds of a gaggle and the distinct, musty scent of hay and feathers. His head throbbed, his mouth tasted like whiskey, and something sharp was digging into his back. He saw the fuzzy figure of a woman quietly gathering eggs. Cole rubbed his head and tried to wipe his eyes clear and steady his vision.

He remembered going to the saloon after speaking with his father at The Grand. He remembered getting into a scrape with Clyde Davis over some ugly remarks he had made, but how he got to Dannah's chicken coop or where the hell Samuel was, he was at a loss.

Samuel, his steed, was a perfect fit for Cole. He stood nearly fifteen hands high. A prize his daddy had bought him when he was still a boy and not nearly big enough for a horse that size or stature. He was dark and noble, like Cole, too. And now when he sat high in the saddle, they looked like a painted pair.

Cole was well over six foot with wavy russet hair that he nearly always covered with a hat. The same hat he's been wearing since he was unable to mount Samuel on his own. Grew into that hat pretty well, too. It eventually allowed his dark but see-through eyes to peek out from under the brim. His eyes gave up his every thought, but his heavy eyelids made them disappear mysteriously when he smiled.

The girls in town made a mash on him. He became a man almost overnight in looks, but he remained a boy in spirit. He loved the games of chasing and hunting as he did when Dannah and him were playmates, which felt so long ago now.

Elisabeth said there wasn't an evil bone in his body, which was amazing seeing who his kin were. But Dannah had often preached at her that his hands weren't clean. He had played a bigger part in their sorrows.

The hedge fence had opened up more than Dannah had imagined. It was not long before Benjamin Hartwell, their neighbor to the north, rode out to meet her. He lent Dannah a couple of his hands with the excuse that he owed her for some mending. His herd was nearly twice hers, yet he had help to spare and even rode up from his cabin to check on her from time to time during the morning.

He lent his ramblers, mostly migrant Mexicans, who traveled from county to county looking to pick up work along the way. Made a good living at $8 a week, when they found a job breaking sod, plowing, or harvesting hay.

Dannah was suspicious of Hartwell's intentions. He was a good twenty years her senior but had his eye on gaining him a wife to mend and cook. Mentioned to Dannah more than once how awful a cook he was, and he always had plenty of suggestions on how to use the Marshall soil, too.

Maybe he was just vying for an invitation to supper or looking for a harmless exchange of troubles, but Dannah feared he was hoping to come to some amicable marital agreement. The way his eyes lingered a second too long on her hands, the way he always found some reason to circle her on horseback, made Dannah wary. She couldn't be certain.

He spoke of soil and seasons, but she could hear what he wasn't saying. A wife to expand his ranch. She wasn't in the market for any of it. But she did, however, know how to handle him, extra flattered by his attention and doubly thankful for his helping hands.

"What are neighbors for?" he'd repeat time and time again, circling her on horseback. She breathed a huge sigh of relief when he finally rode away in the late morning and left her and the hands to their work. She just didn't have it in her today to smile and make conversations-of-no-matter with him.

"Good morning," Elisabeth whispered, glancing back at Cole stirring. He was almost completely submerged in hay; his arms were being held prisoner at his side.

Cole rested his head back onto the ground and stared up at the ceiling. "What in the hell? Lizzie? What … why are you here?" He struggled to lift his head to his chest, and his arms finally followed the command.

"Well, I live here. Oh, and the chickens gave your hiding spot away hours ago," she smiled through her lies, "And shouldn't I be asking you that?"

"Light a shuck, I'm still drunk," he mumbled, growing more awake and more confused.

"I do miss your visits. Would you like to come in for coffee?" Elisabeth frowned, thinking of how she would stretch her supply. She had forgotten the grocer had padded the bag with pebbles.

She disappeared in and out of his vision; he wiped his eyes again. "Me too, Lizzie." He whispered and pulled at the swag chain of his watch.

"I heard you had a book about mythology, you like Greek?"

He stood up and looked around as the barn bowed and rocked under him. It took him a second to get his footing. He brushed his hat out and pulled hay from deep in his pockets. Made his way to the barn door through the throbbing pain in his right thigh, damn near felt like he'd been bitten. He ran his fingers down his leg and found two large holes pierced through his pants, and he winced when he reached through to the skin.

"Cole," he glanced back into the barn at her still plucking eggs, "It was never your fault."

He turned an even more desperate shade of purple and tipped his hat once more before he hobbled off to find Samuel, still rubbing at his thigh.

Elisabeth wanted more than anything to be able to heal his pain — Dannah's, too. To make them hear what she said, to make them see how everything is how it should be. She always had a problem making Cole take notice of her, and some wounds didn't take to needle or thread. Some things had to mend in their own time—if they ever did. She watched him in the distance remove his hat and rub his face back and forth.

CHAPTER EIGHT

It seems as though Benjamin Hartwell had reconsidered being square with Dannah. When she got back to the cabin, he was in the kitchen with his feet propped up, waiting for her. He was patting Queen Esther's head, as if he in fact sat on the throne of the ranch.

"I came by hoping to pay my respects to your mother."

"Oh Dannah, look what Mr. Hartwell has brought, your favorite." Elisabeth gestured to the bouquet on the table.

"They're beautiful," Dannah glanced at the flowers. "I admired them this morning in my kitchen garden Mr. Hartwell." Elisabeth shot Dannah an embarrassed glance. She had made herself almost invisible from her spot behind the stove.

"The flowers?" he asked. "Well, I'm mighty pleased you like them. Late bloomers are always the sweetest," he murmured, his gaze flicking from the flowers to Dannah. "A little patience, and they open right up."

Dannah's whole body tensed. She could feel the blood in her scalp. But she forced her breath steady and let the silence stretch, watching the flicker of unease in his eyes. "I hope you don't mind, I let myself in." Hartwell continued.

"Yes, what are neighbors for," Dannah muttered. Bastard was already stealing from her land, she thought. And where was his horse, perhaps in her corral?

A harmless fellow maybe, but Hartwell was growing annoying. She would refuse his help in the future and would not be so stupid as to extend any open invitations. After all, she almost had everything in place for the season. Rufus, their foreman, had hired some more hands to get things ready for a drive. She still wasn't certain if she would bring the herd up or sell it off locally.

She could still remember the first drive Pa took her on. The painful sores earned from weeks in the saddle. The dirt that never quite came off. The humming of the flankers keeping the herd from straying.

Her pa always made her a pointer at the front with the Mexicans. None of the cowboys ever took to her, black, brown, or white. They barely spoke to her, except for one red-haired vaquero with persistent pink eye, named Alberto. He was from El Paso, and he told Dannah stories of the Salt Wars that drove his family east.

He was excellent on a cutting horse, but he was an odd

stick. He was constantly mumbling to himself, and even when he spoke to others, it was out of the side of his mouth. When he walked, he just seemed to shuffle his heels.

Pa said he was quite the horseman. Said he broke an outlaw bronco that he had all but given up on, and Pa was quite stubborn.

Most of the cowboys were only a bit older than her, but unless they got her confused with the cookie or needed something from the chuck wagon, she was invisible. She knew they thought it best to keep away from the ranch owner's family, but she figured getting paid $20 a month, they would at least acknowledge her.

Elisabeth always said it was best that way. It made it easier to get to Abilene if you settled into the endless miles of solitude. The trek progressed in ten-mile increments.

During the last couple of drives Dannah took with Pa, he started pushing a few miles further than was wise each day in order to keep the herd fat. The fatter ones would fetch $15 more a head. His anxiety about getting back to the ranch and Elisabeth faster always got the better of his patience. Thankfully, their foreman, Rufus, would pull in the reins on their pace when the headcount started to dwindle.

The crew got paid extra for a good drive, and they all looked forward to full pockets when they reached the cattle town and the entertainment it offered. Dannah did not often let herself think of the trail so fancifully, but today she missed it dreadfully. She longed to be away from the ranch for a while.

"Again, I hope you don't mind me coming by Miss Dannah," Hartwell broke in, interrupting her thoughts, "And yes there sure are some late bloomers around here." He said, glancing down at the flowers and then up at Dannah.

"Supper's ready," Elisabeth cut in. She knew her sister could only stand his undertones so long.

"Well something smells delicious in here." Hartwell slapped at his knee and pulled his chair tight into the table. "So how is your mother? Did she cook that up?"

"Oh, she's …" Elisabeth started in.

"Fine, she's fine," Dannah talked over her sister. No use at giving away information Hartwell damn well already knew.

"I'm sorry she couldn't join us. She doesn't do well in this weather." Elisabeth added, waiting patiently for Hartwell to taste his stew.

Out of the corner of her eye, Dannah spotted Hartwell grabbing Elisabeth's hand from her lap. "It's in God's hands now." He began stroking her thumb with his. "It's a wonder she's lasted so long really. Doc says it's a miracle anyone could survive such an ordeal." He reached his other hand toward Dannah.

Dannah stared at his outstretched palm for a long moment and reveled in his discomfort. She turned back to her bowl.

And after another awkward pause, he lowered his hand and began.

"Heavenly Father, thank you for this food we are about to enjoy and for the helping hands, and, of course, the open hearts of our neighbors." And with an "Amen", he once again stretched his hand toward Dannah, this time he wasted no time for reciprocation. He went straight to her shoulder and awkwardly began rubbing it with his fingertips.

Dannah had already begun eating her supper, and his jostling spilled the stew from her spoon. Elisabeth opened her eyes with an affirming Amen, and they ate in silence.

After a while, Hartwell cleared his throat. "Sheriff says they are going to start opening land east of Bastrop. Clear out the last of the Injuns and we'll have ourselves a railroad in no time. Of course, that's if Oxcart John Ireland stays away. Could be as soon as next year though."

Hartwell leaned back, smug. "You know, Miss Dannah, once the line runs clean past San Antonio, they'll need cattle yards at every stop. The Marshall spread would be sittin' real pretty then. You got the land, the herd—hell, with a little help, you could corner the market, a smart woman would get in early."

"And a smarter one wouldn't get in at all," Dannah said, spooning more stew into her mouth, as if to silence him.

Dannah had heard so many stories of the massive rail project. J. Gould, with his Texas and Pacific rail, promised to extend to the Southern Pacific in no time. Of course, the government had palmed him an enormous cash bonus and tax abatement to speed the process up.

Whole towns had picked up and moved to be near the rail up in North Texas. Camp workers spread rumors of bison bones and walls of wool piled high as a hilltop traveling through the prairie at the speed of a pistol shot. It must have been quite the sign of growth.

Traders had gone through the bison herds first for robes, then came back for their tongues, and finally the bones. The bone traders got up to $7 a ton, and everything from dice to china were fashioned from them.

Some found this a blessing. Dannah recalled hearing of Senator Throckmorton's remarks that the sooner the bison died out, the sooner the Indians would get civilized.

Dannah knew of the civilization of which he spoke. She had noticed more and more Indians inside of town, Tonkawa, Lipan, Comanche, and Karankawa. They always looked so strange half-dressed in tribal clothing but capped off with a hat.

The silence was broken again with a strange squeaking in the back of Hartwell's throat as he opened his gullet to the stew. Dannah could actually hear the juices straining through Hartwell's fake teeth.

"Thomas Fowler, at the land office, said we got some real statesmen coming down to these parts to inspire confidence. We'll have ourselves a regular Kansas City before long."

"Mr. Fowler from the land office, and you talk a lot, don't you?" Dannah asked, staring into her raised spoon and pondering what business of hers he might already know.

"Why, yes, he's kin…"

She interrupted again, and her tone intensified dramatically. "So I'm sure you hear plenty 'bout the affairs of most of the folks round here?"

Elisabeth waved a long branch over the table to keep the flies from settling. Dannah had forgotten she was there.

Swallowing even harder, Hartwell shifted high in his chair. "Well, Miss Dannah, if you are asking me about the state of your Daddy's land, I'm afraid I don't know more than you surely do."

"And what exactly is that?" Dannah turned toward him, consciously sweetening her tone. She hated to discuss such matters around Elisabeth, but Hartwell had already tipped his hand. What if he knew something she didn't, and that's why he offered his helping hands today?

"Well, a condemned woman can't be landholder." Hartwell took a big spoonful into his mouth. "Specially if the deed was never in her husband's hands anyhow." He dribbled out a bit of broth from the corner of his mouth.

"My mother is not condemned," Elisabeth said.

"Everyone knows your Ma'd be on the hanging tree, if she could stand long enough to get the noose around her neck. What your Ma did just ain't right. She's lucky Sheriff Hillard is such a Christian man. Lots of people round here think he's a damn fool, letting her live out her days at home and not being brought to justice. Such exceptions aren't usually made."

Dannah calmly let him finish talking. Then she swiftly took up the shotgun and propped it at her right side. She stood and aimed it at Hartwell before he had set his eyes upon her.

"I'm so sorry to be rude Mr. Hartwell, but supper's over." Dannah ran the barrel of her gun down his neck and across his shoulder blade sarcastically.

Hartwell knocked over his chair as he pushed up to his feet, backing his way toward the door. He was still shuffling back carefully, as he stumbled past the porch and slipped down the front steps on his heels.

He let go of a blasting holler, "Dannah Marshall, you have the devil inside you, like your mother. No man will take you and your dying Ma. Not unless they can sleep with their eyes open!"

Elisabeth was in the bedroom checking on Ma. Dannah grabbed the tin with the stolen bouquet from the table and went in to be with her too.

"Look Ma, some daises for you." Dannah placed the flowers by her untouched stew.

"He's right," she sat up a bit in bed. Dannah noticed there were tears filling her eyes. "I am condemned."

"Nonsense," Elisabeth whispered and forced a spoonful toward her. "You can't see your pretty daisies through big teardrops, Mama." She wiped underneath her eyes with her thumb.

Ma didn't flinch or even seem to notice her touch.

"Not for what I did, but for what I failed to do," she looked surprised to make eye contact with Elisabeth, then she stroked her cheek and fell back asleep.

Without a word, Dannah was out of the cabin and mounted on Daisy. By now, the saloon would be full of loud drunkards and loose women. She welcomed the distraction from her troubles.

But by the time she passed Payne's Blacksmith Shop, she had veered east and found herself knocking on Mattie Edward's door, room 13 at The Grand.

Mattie had been brought here like a prize, a woman wrapped in silk and secrets. Dannah didn't know exactly what she was looking for. But maybe—just maybe—she had the answers that whiskey wouldn't give her.

CHAPTER NINE

Mattie threw open the door, half dressed with liquor hot on her breath. She gave Dannah a subtle grin of recognition and stepped behind the door to let her in. "I have been expecting you. Maybe not at so formal an hour, but I knew you'd come."

She closed up her robe in a false gesture of modesty as she rolled back onto the sofa, exposing herself once again. She was as confident as when Dannah saw her strolling around town in full Sunday dress, but reddened pox marks framed her face now instead of rouge. And they followed a trail down her neck to where her thin nightgown revealed blistering and oozing.

"How's your Mama? I'm sure she's feeling much better these days." She answered herself. "Few more weeks of rest, and she'll be good as new."

She flashed a sympathetic smile, and Dannah recognized the faint remnants of her beauty, but noticed she had bald spots scattered all over her scalp. She shook when she poured a glass of Old Nick's that Dannah refused.

She took up the drink for herself and tucked her feet under the sofa cushions. "So why did you come to me? To hear when I think the rain will stop or what I've heard about the newest New York fashions?"

Silence fell between them except for the noises coming from the street.

"I know you blame your Daddy for cheating on your Ma, but truth is he was one of the good ones. I'll be gone soon," Her tone changed from arrogant to serious, and she rushed the last of the words out of her mouth as if she were spitting them.

"I'm not interested in rewriting history today, Mattie." Dannah interjected, but it didn't seem to matter.

"He didn't start up with me because he didn't love your mother. He came to me for help with Henry. I was a last-ditch effort, I suppose."

"Funny. The version I got didn't mention you being the savior type," Dannah came back at her.

"We talked about how much he loved all of his girls," her tone was dismissive now, "and how much it tore him up that he was gonna lose everything. I couldn't help him with his debt. And I sure couldn't make Henry take back their dealings. Truthfully, I never asked the son of a bitch." She said flippantly.

"It wouldn't have mattered." She dismissed herself. "Your pa was terrified of losing it all, and I think he found comfort in me. Until he didn't care no more. I can be a nice distraction for a troubled man. He told me things, fears that he couldn't tell your Ma. He didn't want to let her down. Maybe he was getting back at Henry for the ordeal the bastard was putting him through.

Hell, maybe I was getting revenge, too. I've never claimed to be the most faithful wife, but till your Daddy, I had stuck to becoming friendly with only passersby in this Godforsaken place.

But the first time I heard your Daddy talk about your Ma; I had to feel that version of love. For a moment, to feel it settle upon my skin even if it wasn't for me."

"It wasn't yours to feel." Dannah interrupted.

"Maybe I thought I could borrow it, just for a while. Maybe I thought I deserved a piece of something good. Course, things weren't so clear at the time. Clarity is so very fleeting, don't last longer than fifteen minutes."

Mattie shifted back against the sofa cushion and crossed her arms tight across her chest.

"He was a good man with some weakness before the sickness took over. But after, the daddy you knew was dead. It came quick, too. He could have lived years without disturbing his head like it did. Maybe God decided to speed things along, because he was a good man in his past life with you all. The doctors say I've been exceedingly lucky."

She drew in a huge, wheezy breath. "I could go on like this for years. But they're wrong. I'm the one being punished."

Dannah just listened to her ramble, as if she could possibly excuse what her father had done. It completely infuriated Dannah that she ignored her part in it all—just sat there completely at peace with her deeds, believing that her hell was already in service.

But Dannah listened. Mattie had a way of commanding attention, and not only by men. Besides, there was no use in trying to convince someone of their own sins.

She was a woman who was always being watched and always putting on a show. She was that woman an artist wanted to sketch, like in one of Elisabeth's drawing books. She had something that called out, even to Dannah.

It must have been tiresome, Dannah thought, relieved that she could slip into a room without all eyes going on her. Dannah drifted in and out of Mattie's conversation.

Dannah conjured her ma and daddy dancing around the cabin in the early mornings. He used to swing her around the table, tangled up in his arms. The tips of her toes barely skimmed the ground. Dannah saw them clear as day—her nightdress fanning out like a cloud. He always made her feel weightless. They had the kind of love that didn't carry burdens, that didn't make excuses. The kind that felt solid. Dannah hadn't thought about that in years. Hadn't let herself. But now, standing in Mattie Edwards' whiskey-soaked room, it hit her like a slap.

He'd ask Elisabeth for a turn or two, and then he and Dannah would make off before sunrise. Daniel would make them stop on the way home, no matter how tired or hungry they were, to pick a flower for Mama. He always told Dannah, "If a man ever forgets to thank you after a dance, it didn't matter how clean his nails are, he's no proper fellow." Mama would still be singing when they'd get back at night.

At bedtime, they used to tell the story of how they met at the fundraiser for Texas A&M University. Mama's father was set to be a teacher in Austin, and he moved the family down from Tennessee. But until the new University of Texas opened, he attached himself to any higher institute of education he could.

Everybody who was anybody came to these fundraisers. The whole state must have been there, but Daniel saw Clare from across the room and asked her to share her peach cobbler.

The way Ma told it, he'd strolled right up to her and said he was real sorry, but he'd gotten so distracted by her that he'd dropped his on the floor. So he figured it was only fair that she owed him a taste.

She, of course, let him eat the whole piece except for the very last bite. She said the last bite was hers and flashed her smile at him just as he was scooping it up with his spoon. But like a gentleman, he said that was his plan all along, anyway.

Mattie continued on. She spoke like a woman confessing without asking forgiveness. It made Dannah's teeth grind. She didn't need excuses. Didn't need to hear about "fleeting clarity" or "Godforsaken places." She needed the truth, but the truth sounded too much like weakness, and she had no use for that.

"You want forgiveness, Mattie?" Dannah said, standing. "Start with telling the truth like it costs you something."

Mattie lifted her glass. "That's the thing about the truth, sweetheart. It usually costs you everything." She shot a sly glance at Dannah. "Is that what you're trying to find with Cole?"

Dannah narrowed her eyes. "You don't know a damn thing."

"Secrets have a way of catching up with everyone, especially pretty ones with guns and guilt."

Dannah got up and left Mattie on the sofa, still explaining life with a fresh pour in hand. She had all the answers she needed from Mattie Edwards. She had made a mistake in going to room thirteen at The Grand. She didn't stop at the saloon on the way home as she intended either; somehow, drunkards and loose women didn't seem good company anymore.

CHAPTER TEN

Dannah left early the next morning to make her way to San Antonio, to get an estimate on the herd and to pick up some supplies.

Rufus was by the corral checking the shoes on one of the new geldings when Dannah approached. His weathered hands moved slow but sure, as if every hoof he touched told him a story.

"You heard of a man talking like he already owned what ain't his?" she asked, arms folded, watching the horse's flank rise and fall.

Rufus gave a grunt. "Hartwell?"

She nodded.

"He been sniffin' round the trailhands too. Asking about headcounts. Grazing rights."

"He'll get neither," Dannah said.

Rufus spat into the dirt and leaned back. "He's a politician dressed like a neighbor. Careful with men like that. They don't use rope to take your land—they use ink."

Dannah looked out toward the ridge, the outline of their herd drifting like smoke. "Then maybe it's time we pushed the herd north. I want that stock on the move before the next moonrise."

"Yes, ma'am," Rufus said, but his eyes narrowed. "This ain't just business, is it?"

"It never is," she muttered. She mounted Daisy, her pale mare with a coat like fog just before sunrise—soft, dappled, and always seeming a breath away from vanishing into the landscape. Age had freckled her muzzle and dimmed her gallop, but she was still sure-footed as ever, with the kind of memory that could trace old creek beds in the dark. Her mane, long and wispy, caught the light like linen on a clothesline, and her eyes held that steady, unreadable calm that only came from years on the trail.

Daisy wasn't fast anymore, especially with wagon in tow, but she was faithful—weathered and like Dannah still moving forward, even when everything else wanted to turn back.

It was two full days ride into the city, but well worth it. Henry Edwards and a couple of his men had control of prices around Medea.

She was about the only one except a couple of Mexican tenant farmers that didn't buy chicken feed and sell crop and cattle through him.

For most folks, it wasn't a choice. Cross him, and the

next time you needed grain, the stores were suddenly empty. The next time you needed credit, the bank doors stayed shut. She'd heard stories of cattle vanishing in the night, of crops mysteriously set ablaze. But Dannah found no greater pleasure than spitting in the eye of a man who thought himself untouchable.

The trail from Medea to San Antone was scattered with price-gouging outposts and a couple ranches, but mostly it was the endless hills and valleys that made it seem to last forever.

When she was little, her father would pick the lowest-hanging cloud and swear they could catch it if they rode hard enough. She believed him for a while. Even when the clouds shifted, she'd pretend they were just barely out of reach. It took her longer than she cared to admit to realize the chase was impossible.

Now, as she rode alone, she no longer chased clouds. She just watched them drift, untethered, untouchable.

She loved when the clouds looked like they grazed the hilltop. And at every hilltop they reached, she'd revel in the moment before her eyes completely focused and wonder if they would see anyone meandering down in the valley. It was like unwrapping a package. Of course, if they had seen anyone, she'd have to hide and make her gun ready.

The ride took a lot out of Daisy these days, but Dannah knew how to pace a good mare—frequent halts, loose reins, and never too long between sips of stream water. By the time they neared the end though, Daisy was enjoying the change of scenery as much as Dannah. Nice to stretch her stiff legs past Medea every now and then to see what they were actually capable of. The days were already getting longer, but Dannah decided to make camp just shy of town and start fresh in the morning.

She rode to a familiar patch of forest that Pa and her always used to camp. It was the perfect plush patch of ground protected by a sweeping circle of giant oaks. She used to try to wrap her arms around them, but they were always too massive. She didn't try this time.

Pa had said it used to be Tonkawan gathering grounds until the tribe was scattered by a push from Coffee's infamous Rangers.

Some of the tribes were pushed into Oklahoma, and some to the east to lessen the ground they had to defend against, or they were herded into the panhandle and Fort Sill.

Not many outside of central Texas remembered Coffee Hays, but he had commanded men in the Republic's heyday who specialized in quick raids, brutal ambushes, and clearing land by whatever means necessary. Folks called it progress. Others called it blood theft. Her pa never quite said, but he always checked for ashes, bones, discarded moccasins. "Don't disrespect a ghost by sleeping on its grave," he used to say.

Pa also checked for living threats and made sure there hadn't been any fresh fires or food before he'd let Dannah dismount Daisy.

She did the same now. The Austin paper said fifty

whites had been kidnapped by Indian renegades last year alone. They raided forts and camps.

She remembered hearing the scary stories of a young white girl, Cynthia Ann something, who had been ripped away from her family by Comanches. She was found twenty-five years later married to the chief himself; she even had his children. The story had made Elisabeth cry. She said it was such a strange tragedy. The poor thing didn't even remember how to speak English or her God-given name.

Parker sounded right to Dannah, but Elisabeth would know for sure. Her sister had often said it wasn't right; this girl being taken from her family twice in one lifetime. To not know if they were out there, alive or dead, to yearn, and to wonder if she would be forgotten.

After a couple of circles, Dannah determined the camp to be safe and there were no signs anyone had been there in some time. With all the lodging popping up all around the state, not as many people were sleeping around a fire anymore. Dannah gathered up some kindling and dried grass and then took out the rabbit she'd caught earlier. She would have herself a feast fit for an old warrior ghost tonight.

San Antonio had changed. Hotels weren't just rooms over a saloon or bunks behind a general store anymore. They had names now—grand names. The Menger, the Maverick, the Dullnig. The kind of places that served brandy in cut glass and hired German butlers who looked down their noses at muddy boots. She didn't stay at those.

But she took a good long look from the outside. She remembered when hotels had more fleas than guests. Now, they had dining rooms, telephones in the lobby, and little brass bells you rang for bathwater.

It made her wonder if the West was getting domesticated one white linen tablecloth at a time.

The visit into San Antonio was a wretched one. Dannah got fleeced on some seed prices, but she made a contract with a vaquero named Ernesto from the Darling Ranch. She'd sell the herd to him for a discounted rate per head, and he'd bring them through the stretch and into Denison rail along with his sheep and Angora goats. In return for the discount, he'd bring her back twenty head of breeding stock shorthorns. The Herefords particularly, and the shorthorns, were supposed to be less susceptible to the cattle tick.

"Ticks and ink," she muttered. "That's what's killin' Texas now."

She kept her ears open for news to bring home to Elisabeth—one of the few luxuries her sister still asked for. That and one of Edison's strange new light bulbs, or a telephone, "if it weren't too much trouble."

They had heard of these baffling inventions from newspaper clippings their grandfather had sent from Austin. The way Elisabeth spoke of them, as if they'd bring civilization straight to their doorstep, made Dannah uneasy.

The news came like wind from all directions—loud, fast, full of dust and little certainty. Dannah caught quite a few stories from Ernesto concerning the rail. Henry Villard's Northern Pacific and, of course, Mr. Long, "winning the west without a single shot." A grand celebration of the rail's new path into Bismarck was honored by the presence of the Crow reservation, and Sitting Bull himself delivered a speech. The rousing words seemed to gather mixed reviews from what Dannah could ascertain, but Sitting Bull's translator was rumored to be drunk as hell.

Ernesto shook his head and said, "One minute they hate the tribes, next minute they clap when they speak. You tell me what that means." She didn't have an answer.

He spoke too of barbed wire—the kind of talk that made cowmen grit their teeth. Fences going up fast, rivers cut off, roads gone from maps. Men in Menard County were losing their minds over it, cutting fence by night with wire nippers and vengeance. "They're calling it a war now," Ernesto said, sipping his mezcal. "I saw a barn burnt over it. Whole herd of horses torched in the stall."

"Wouldn't be the first time blood got spilled over wire," Dannah said. "Johnny Ringo made his bones during the Mason County War—over a handful of stolen cattle and too much barbed fence."

Dannah wondered if anyone from the Jones family had been part of that blaze. There were whispers about them —too many cousins, too many grudges, too much whiskey.

Ernesto also told her of the Chinese miners killed after the Chinese Exclusion Act was enforced and their American citizenship hopes were revoked. Mumblings of the

Catholics rallying for James S. Hogg. About some cattle baron building a fancy new hotel in Austin called The Driskill and the rancher Charles Goodnight foolishly paying Quanah Parker not to hunt his buffalo herd. Dannah remembered the name Quanah Parker. Quanah was the son of Cynthia Ann Parker, the white woman who had been kidnapped by the Comanche. Dannah knew Elisabeth would be over the moon with all this rich news, but it exhausted Dannah.

She ventured into the closest saloon. She wondered why everyone talked about Charles Goodnight as if he were a fool. He was, after all, savvy enough to buy up all the land he could after the war. Obviously, he knew a little something about commerce.

She learned more news of some buffalo soldiers being lynched while serving at Fort Concho from a man waiting for the wagon wheeler. Apparently, the man had gotten into the spirits last night and hadn't soaked his wheels. He didn't discover they had shrunk up on him until he was moving, and they came clean off.

Dannah rode home beaten from the trip and reeling from all the world's goings-on outside the walls of Medea. To Daisy's dismay, the wagon was filled with sorghum, sulfur, black tea, and cement. Dannah's mind was heavy too with thoughts of how she'd manage the ranch.

How was she going to make enough money to keep it running, even if she did get the deed in her hand finally? Selling preserves would certainly not be enough, nor would doing laundry for the rumored rail workers they awaited.

The deal with Ernesto sat heavy in her gut. Selling the herd meant staying home. Staying home meant feeling the walls of the ranch close in tighter. The trail was freedom, the only place where the weight of Medea and Henry Edwards and land disputes couldn't touch her. But she couldn't leave Elisabeth and Ma—not this year. She told herself it was the right choice. That didn't mean she liked it.

Besides, she didn't have the money to pay the picked-over cowboys she had already hired for field work. And with the rail expanding, it would hardly be worth the strife soon enough. Well, maybe she'd still be able to bring the cattle in next year; she truly longed for the solitude of the trail.

On her second night out, the wind changed. The kind of change that sent animals restless, that made the world feel different even before the first crack of thunder. She pushed Daisy harder; the storm was coming from the north. No campfire rituals, no comforts tonight—just stop after stop, letting Daisy catch her wind while the storm gathered behind them.

She knew they wouldn't be home until after midnight, but the dark wouldn't slow them much, as they knew these parts well. A strange cold settled into Dannah's bones and swam about her head. She had the uneasy feeling she wasn't just outriding a storm. She was riding straight into one.

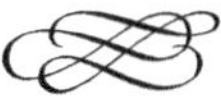

"Son of a bitch." Dannah catapulted off Daisy as she neared the cabin, tying the reins to the tree with one downward sweeping motion on the branch. She quietly snuck up behind the man at her window. Thank God old Queeny would be snoring by now and not give her away.

She swung all her weight to the side, twisting at the waist, and hit him with the rifle butt. Billy buckled to the ground.

"Why, Billy, what a pleasant surprise." Dannah gave his crumbled silhouette a tiny curtsy.

She peered into an empty house. She scanned the room again to find Elisabeth fast asleep in her chair, her finger still marking a page in her book.

Dannah looked down at the crumpled boy on her porch. She certainly wasn't going to carry another Edwards boy to safety. She found herself entertaining the thought of pouring his blood just enough to tempt an animal into finishing the job. But she didn't want any big creatures to learn it was okay to approach the cabin, so she hesitantly settled on leaving Billy intact.

After unsaddling Daisy, she went inside with an accomplished feeling from her long trip after all. She heaved a huge storing trunk against the door and went straight to bed.

First thing the next morning, Dannah peered out the window to check for any signs of Billy left from their midnight rendezvous.

"Elisabeth, will you finish mending those curtains? It's hotter now and you know how Queeny hates to wake up before breakfast gets underway." Dannah headed for the coffee, giving Queeny a pat as she passed. Queeny smiled all tongue and spit, ready for Elisabeth to drop a morsel of egg, anything.

"Ma took a turn for the worse while you were gone. She hasn't eaten since you left. Maybe she'll eat for you?"

"Do I need to call on Doc Olsen?" Dannah asked, heading for her parent's old bedroom.

"No more tonics, she needs her strength, she needs to eat," She brought a bowl of vegetable soup and spoon to Dannah.

Her vision pulsed at the edges, narrowing into a tunnel. She reached for something—anything—to steady herself, but her fingers found only air. The soup sloshed over the rim of the bowl, and then the bowl itself vanished from her grip. She barely registered the sharp crack of her head against the chair. She could feel Elisabeth leaving the cabin. She could feel the cold metal spoon in her fingertips. She could feel the ground under her. Then nothing.

Cole was knee high in the river, attending to his early morning fishing when he heard Queeny's yelping coming closer. "Whoa, whoa" he yelled out, but Queeny didn't stop.

He was mounted on Samuel within seconds and headed for the Marshall's, his fishing pole still in hand. He stormed into the cabin without a knock to find Dannah still on the floor.

"You're soaking wet," he said to an unconscious Dannah, picking her up from beside the wood stove. "I have to get your fever down."

He placed Dannah on the bed and sat next to her. Queeny came in a minute or two after him. "You did a good job, girl."

Cole found that there was a basin of water and towels by her bed. She must have been feeling badly before this. He placed a wet towel on her forehead and left her side to fetch Doc Olsen. Hours passed. Dannah did not stir. But she felt Elisabeth refresh her towel every so often.

When Cole finally returned with the Doc, he said Dannah would be fine, when they got the fever to break.

"She is worn thin. I don't think she went and picked up anything in the city, but it would do good to watch her temperature closely. Her trip and the heat, it just seems like exhaustion."

While he was there, he checked in on Ma. After he'd

shut her door behind him, he whispered to Cole, "That dog's watchin' her close, doin' her part. But she won't hold out long—'specially runnin' dry. If you can, see if she'll take a little water, maybe a bite. Just enough to ease her some."

Dannah could feel the prairie grass-stuffed mattress soaked through under her. She could feel herself drift in and out, like a bird soaring through deep treetops. Unsure if the waking moments were blue sky or dark canopy, except for when she heard familiar voices.

Face down and strapped upon a dark horse, she was folded over the hindquarters as if she were getting ready for a wallop. She could still feel the animal's weight shift through her own ribs from the rear left to the right and back again. Her hands were bound to the saddle and her legs to each other at the ankle. When she felt a slap come down upon the horse, she remembered thrusting all her weight to her shoulders by digging the toe of her boots into the horse's spongy side. She could still see the ground disappearing; it too rushed alongside them, chasing the river water.

"Help her, help her!" Dannah screamed over and over, looking down at her mother.

She searched the crowd for a face that wasn't empty, for someone who might step forward. And then she saw him—Cole. Standing still, watching her go. His mouth didn't open. His hands didn't reach. He just watched.

She was screaming out for Cole to help her ma. She begged for him to help, but he didn't. She saw all the townspeople just standing together in neat little rows, like they were watching a stage play. The audience got smaller and further away. She felt a tight grasp upon her back, a fist full of her shirt and skin in Hillard's hand keeping her mounted atop the horse.

A moment of blue sky and a cloth to her head, and a hand stroking her hair. And she was out again, back at the banks that day.

Her ears burned with the brushing of her mother below. Her ma's screams stopped, and she was silent now. All she can hear is the thrashing of hooves, the rushing water, the snapping of branches, and the occasional "Hi-yah!" sucked inward by the rider accompanied by a kick into the horse's ribs. Dannah shook every time she heard a crack from below because she knew there was a good chance that it was her mother's bones and not a tree branch. Silence grew deeper and lower inside her. But she still gasped in each time her ma's face plowed into a root or overturned a rock. And when she couldn't watch anymore, she saw Cole's face again, just watching her ride away.

She drifted awake, her vision hazy, but she saw him— Cole, on his knees, head bowed like a man at prayer. His lips moved, but she couldn't hear him. Maybe he wasn't speaking to her at all. Maybe he was speaking to the ghost of her mother, to the version of himself that had done nothing when she needed him most. He held the very same expression that he had given her when Mama was being dragged along the river Medea.

Out again.

A year had passed since the dragging, but still she bore the rope scars upon her wrists, and now the cabin was haunted with the breathing ghost of her mother that lived in her parents' old bedroom. It once was a happy place.

Dannah opened her eyes. They stuck back together again. Cole was still there by her side. She wasn't sure how much time had passed, but by the look of the number of rags by her bed, it had been a while. She had mustered enough strength to think straight and to shake the vivid memories of the dragging. She lay there for a long time, eyes shut until she felt him get up and leave again.

She sat up fast, forcing her skin to peel away from the brittle bed, and searched the floor over for her clothes. The room spun around her.

The door opened again. Cole must have heard her making noise. He stopped in his tracks, realizing the bed was empty. "You gave us quite a scare..." His eyes widened upon seeing Dannah was only half dressed. "You're up." He sputtered.

"Get back in bed, you need your ..." He tried to look away, but Dannah whipped up her rifle and laid it across her bare chest. She couldn't find her shirt but always knew where her gun was. She had the barrel aimed at him before he had come all the way through the door. Cole froze, his mouth parting, but no sound came out for a few awkward moments.

"Dannah," he reached a hand out toward her, "Do you

know what happened? You are ill. Put that down and get back into bed."

She felt a cold rush down her spine and a sweat break out into her eyes. "Why, Cole? Why?"

He shook his head. He didn't understand her question. Or maybe he really did, but he still looked at her with a cocked head like Queeny often did. He watched her slight standing sways from the heel to ball of her foot and back again.

Cole took in a deep breath. "Do you remember that time when we were kids," he inched toward Dannah, "and you decided you was gonna get a peach from the Wilkinson's orchard if it killed you? You said you had a craving for it, and you wouldn't let it go. You remember what happened?"

He waited for her response, but all she gave were slow, long blinks and more swaying, but her rifle remained aimed squarely at him.

"Mr. Wilkinson almost shot you dead, must've thought you was a straggler. I ain't never seen somebody run so fast in my life, but you never let go of that peach, didn't even bruise it neither. To this day, I can't even smell a peach without thinking of you climbing up to fetch it and hanging from that tree by your feet like a damn possum and grinning like you'd won the world." His voice softened. "You never let go of that peach. Didn't even bruise it."

But she wasn't grinning now. She was swaying; the rifle slipping lower. And with that, she was out. Cole jolted forward, trying to reach her before she hit the ground, but he didn't. He lifted her onto the bed and breathed a sigh of relief that the gun hadn't gone off when she fell. It still lay cradled in her arms like her baby.

Two hours passed before she woke up again for good this time. Cole was still there, but her rifle and pistol were both missing. He was certain that her fever was gone this time, as her threats increased in coherency. But he didn't tell her where her guns were until he was out the front door, at a safe distance past the well. He yelled to her, "In your dowry chest. Somehow I knew you'd never look there!"

She retrieved them, brushing aside the crispy linens, which bore deep yellowed edges. "Dannah, where are you going? Doc said you need to rest," Elisabeth stopped sweeping the cabin ground and yelled after her through the door.

"I'll be back real soon." Dannah said, with boots still in one hand, lifting the empty arm to wave, but she didn't turn back to explain further.

CHAPTER TWELVE

illy eagerly met Cole outside their cabin. "Pa's been looking everywhere for you. Even went into town to see if you'd picked up a whore or something."

"I was helping out the Marshalls. Dannah's had a little spell."

"So you wuz with a whore. Deserves everything she gets," Billy mumbled.

"Shut up, Billy, unless you want to visit Doc, too." Cole walked past Billy, slamming the door in his face.

Billy followed, almost skipping after him. "You know, Cole, you're right. I have to be more neighborly. Maybe I'll bring a little something over and make her feel better. I mean, she's done with you, maybe I'll have a go at the gal."

Henry Edwards' home was filled with outdated knickknacks and portraits of Parisian street scenes, like a storefront window. For their first year there as man and wife, Mattie had brought in all the comforts of home from up north. Even ordered special silver spoons that still hung on the wall.

Henry had left everything as she had decorated it. Even her desk still held a stack of the stationery that she received as a wedding gift from his Aunt Cora in New York City. It read Mr. & Mrs. Henry Edwards and was surrounded by tiny royal blue calla lilies, only the finest for the new bride.

At first, Mattie had only spent part of the week in town. Soon she'd stopped coming to church with her husband on Sundays. He was humiliated. There were rumors of her fragility and her constitution, but they were silenced when she got pregnant with Cole. Folks figured their marriage was good enough to have children and were surprised she was strong enough to live through it. But as soon as the boys were old enough to walk, she left them at the ranch full time along with all her wonderful city things.

She had it pretty good though, Dannah had tagged along with Cole for many visits to the hotel. She always had ribbon candy and chocolate to offer them. She said they were the boss candy, the finest they would ever have and doled them out a half-piece each. Yes, Henry gave her a real nice setup. She was ace-high, why would she ever leave him to go back north a marked woman?

Cole focused back on Billy, who was nearly chest to chest with him now. "You've been defending Dannah Marshall since you was little, Cole, but she hates you," Billy leaned even closer.

"Why do you think that is? Because you just watched her mama being whipped, because you caused it all with your little secrets, or maybe you just weren't man enough for her? Maybe she wasn't satisfied with you?"

Cole was on him like a wild dog. He forgot himself and suddenly tore into Billy's stomach, relentlessly slamming him back against the wall so hard the portraits rattled. He didn't think—just drove his fists into Billy's gut, over and over, each impact sending shockwaves up his arms. Billy grunted, tried to twist away.

He only stopped after he felt a punch upon his left side that was far stronger than Billy could have delivered. It was their father ripping the boys apart.

Henry moved like a shadow—silent, swift. One of his father's hands had Billy by the throat, the other pressing cold and firm against Cole's chest, like a steel bar pinning him in place. He didn't need to say anything to part the brothers. His grip was enough to remind them both who owned them.

"Look at this place. You don't have any respect. You broke your mother's table." He pointed at it on the ground.

"It's not Mother's table. It was never Mother's table. She sat at it once in the past eight years. She ain't ever coming back here. Not for a visit, not to live, nuthin'." Cole regretted the words as soon as they were out of his mouth. It was Billy's turn to rush at Cole. But instead, Billy rammed his daddy across the chest by mistake, throwing him to the ground with a massive thud.

Both the boys stopped throwing punches and froze. They were on the floor too, and neither one took their eyes off their father, waiting for his next move. Henry Edwards slowly stood up, but the boys remained very still.

Henry stepped forward, slow and deliberate, planting his boot against Cole's chest. He pressed down—gently at first, then harder. The pressure built, stealing Cole's breath inch by inch. He stayed still, teeth grinding, refusing to let his father see him gasp.

"You put a stop to this. Fix your mother's table," Henry said, adding just a little more weight before finally stepping back. "And then get to the fence materials."

He took the toe of his boot to Cole's chin and forced his head to the side, so he could see the table lying in pieces on the floor. He left their cabin as calmly and quietly as he had come in.

CHAPTER THIRTEEN

*H*enry Edwards swaggered into the saloon for a visit before he went across to see his wife. He knew better than to go over unannounced, not that he'd ever admit it. Maybe he didn't even realize it—but he'd made a habit of visiting at the same time each day, never making the mistake of just dropping in.

Saloon activities still halted when Henry Edwards entered, Dannah they grew accustomed to, but they'd never feel at ease in Edwards' presence. Laughter dulled, shoulders tensed, conversations steered clear of anything risky. He wasn't sheriff, but he was the one men feared when they had debts they couldn't pay. The ones who owed him knew better than to make a scene—they just melted into the walls or made a slippery farewell out the back door.

Sheriff Hillard pulled up a stool next to Edwards.

"John," Edwards acknowledged him, but continued to stare straight into his ale.

"Here's how!" the Sheriff raised his glass at Edwards.

Henry did not reciprocate the toast. "People around here been talking about you needing to hand over your badge, John."

"What people?" Hillard asked wide-eyed and wounded from the offense.

"People whose opinions matter. They are saying you ain't got the stomach for it no more." He continued ignoring Hillard's inquiry. "This has always been a quiet town and you've done good keeping the peace. But we've got more and more Mexicans movin' back up here, and soon the rail's gonna be bringin' in more settlers. Our future depends on the strong hand of the law."

"I've always ..." Hillard's brow furrowed down, and he leaned into Henry Edwards to protest, but the Sheriff lost his balance and fumbled off the stool. He caught himself with both elbows smack atop the bar but knocked his ale down the length of the counter.

"John," Henry's voice dipped into something just shy of pity. "You can't even bring in a known murderess. I've been more than patient, but I want my land, and I want the Marshall women to stop raising hell around here. Maybe the boys in Austin are right—maybe you don't have the stomach for it anymore."

Hillard stiffened, jaw clenching. "Who the hell says that?"

Henry took a slow sip of ale. "Men whose decisions

carry weight." He shrugged, like it wasn't personal. "You let a woman make you look like a fool. And now I've got the land commissioner breathing down my neck because you can't handle a little girl." His tone turned from demanding to nearly sympathetic sounding. "Hell, Johnny, it should be a cinch. I've got your sworn testimony as a lawman and the bitch don't even have the deed. Daniel Marshall never got it in his hands after his five was up. That should stop any questions from the state. But they must think you're a joke."

Edwards shot down the rest of his ale and gave a hard slap to the Sheriff's back, sending him stomach first into the bar again. He sauntered out of the saloon, across the street for Mattie's.

Back at the Edwards Ranch, Billy had, of course, angled toward the door before his father was out of sight. Before he left, he paused long enough to smirk at Cole.

"Reckon you're gonna fix that table, huh?"

"Somebody's got to."

"Ain't gonna be me. Pa never blamed me for anything anyhow."

"No, he just leaves me the mess and lets you run wild."

"Don't be sore," Billy called, already halfway out the door. "I'll be back to help eat supper. Maybe."

Cole clenched his jaw but said nothing. The table leg wobbled like his hands.

Billy was off to waste the day with no qualms of leaving Cole to clean up the havoc. Cole felt the sting of jealousy rise up in him. Billy, however rotten he was, had freedom from his father. Billy had never felt the heavy burden against his chest or of his father's boot for that matter.

Cole hammered the first nail into the solid oak leg of his mother's table. He had a hazy recollection of sitting with her at that table. Billy wouldn't remember the presence of his mother in the house at all, yet another thorn in Cole's side. What bliss not to be haunted by what once was, he thought. His father also seemed to be a different person back then, or perhaps Cole was too young to know any better.

Cole remembered riding with his parents to the gospel mill, trying not to get his Sunday clothes dirty. Dannah always wore a sky-blue ribbon in her hair on Sundays, and she'd whisper prayers that didn't match the ones spoken aloud. She'd sit up straight, feet swinging above the floor, her little hymnal always upside down. Cole could still hear the voices, feel his mother's hand smoothing the wrinkles from his Sunday best, smell the faint lavender she dabbed behind her ears. His father's voice boomed next to him, the loudest in the congregation —besides Preacher Menard, that is. He had believed it, then. That they were good. That they were whole. And then the memory shifted.

Blessed assurance, Jesus is mine!
O what a foretaste of glory divine!
Heir of salvation, purchase of God,
Born of His spirit, washed in His blood.
This is my story, this is my song,

Praising my Savior all the day long.

When Preacher Menard's voice would crack on the high notes, it used to tickle Cole and Dannah so much. Got to the point where Dannah couldn't even look at Cole from across the way—it would send them both into wild giggles and, of course, get them into their fair share of trouble. Menard used to say he was kin to that Frenchman Michel Menard, the one who helped found Galveston. Folks figured that's why he wore silk socks and a silver pocket watch even when he preached in the woods. Many Sundays, many lazy afternoons later, and they wouldn't share any secret jokes or even a passing hello.

At first, Dannah didn't look over at Cole anymore when everyone bowed their heads to pray. But he still watched her, and she knew it, too. She could always feel his eyes were upon her. It used to feel like the sun beating down on her cheeks, real comforting like family, but now it burned on the inside of her skin.

"Cole, what's wrong with you?" He remembered she had once asked him. "We ain't gone scavenging in weeks. Are you mad at me? Is it your Ma, has she gone ill again?"

"Nah, I just have a lot to do, Dan. Mavericks need branding yet and I can only do fifteen cows an hour by myself, not counting notching …" He could still remember the sinking feeling that settled in his stomach lying to her for the first time. He couldn't tell her what was really wrong. He didn't even understand the way he was feeling after what had happened.

Pa had said he had a birthday gift for Cole and took

him to the saloon for a drink. Cole had tasted his father's ale before, but whiskey was a whole different story. It was disgusting, Cole thought. It must have been like licking the back of the outhouse. It burned his throat all the way down into his stomach, to parts of his insides he didn't think he'd felt before. It made him feel inside out.

Afterwards, his father led Cole down the alleyway and stopped close to the back of the general store. He swiftly opened a small door and ushered the boy inside a narrow room with no windows and said only, "I'll be back in a bit."

He gave his son a shove forward by the shoulder before he shut the door behind him. Cole noticed the stale little room was fairly empty except for a bureau pulled in front of the inside door and a bed with a strange woman upon it. She seemed to be expecting them.

Cole had never seen this woman in the town before. After a few moments passed, he asked the woman lying upon her stomach, legs V'd corner-to-corner across the bed, "Who are you?"

"I'm a friend of your Daddy's," She motioned to him with an open palm, but Cole didn't budge. "Said it was your birthday. Is that so?" She slid off the bed and crouched down next to Cole.

"Yes ma'am it is."

"And how old are you?"

Cole didn't answer her. He was stumped at what he was doing here. She continued in a low voice, "Happy birthday, sweetheart. Well, shoot, luke, or give up the gun," she stroked Cole across the chest.

He didn't know what to do. He looked toward the door frantically. "You're okay, darling. Come over here and let me give you a present."

Cole cringed when he smelt her get close and again when her calloused hands began to touch him. He kept his eyes shut the whole time she sat on top of him. She must have outweighed him by fifty pounds, and he gasped aloud a couple of times when he couldn't catch his breath. Cole didn't understand what was happening to him; she took control. He heard her cackle at him, but he still didn't open his eyes. He didn't get his wind back for ten minutes, and when he did, he quickly got up from the bed, straightened up, and wiped his cheeks dry.

"What's wrong darlin'? I got the proof, that you enjoyed yourself."

Cole stood silently waiting, cemented to the corner of the bureau that sat against the wall. The woman carefully rolled a quirley and lit it. It would be another fifteen minutes before his father came back through the doorway. He very carefully unfolded a stack of bills from his pocket.

"I'll see you real soon Doris." He threw the bills at the woman, who was again sprawled across the bed.

"Doris," Cole said to himself. He'd heard the name once before—whispers from townsfolk that she'd been kicked out of the Chicken Ranch down in La Grange. That place had been running since the Civil War, a so-called 'boarding house' with a velvet parlor and a line of customers longer than Sunday service. But even they had rules. If Doris got tossed from there, she must've broken every one.

She replied nothing, but had the money tucked away in her corset and another cigarette lit before the door closed.

When they had turned from the alley into the main street, he pulled Cole toward him by the shoulder and said, "Now you're a man. You understand?" Cole nodded out of habit. He didn't understand anything that just happened. It hadn't hurt, but he didn't like Doris; she was foul, almost scary.

"Be expecting more from you. But I couldn't very well give you the responsibilities of a man without giving you some of the privileges."

They continued walking. "You won't be goin' to school no more either. I'll teach you all you need. We have real business to do. Tell me you understand, boy."

"Yes sir, I understand." Cole lied.

CHAPTER FOURTEEN

Even as they grew apart that summer, Dannah had noticed Cole staring at her in church again. It was different; he wasn't trying to mouth a joke at her as he had in their youth. He just stared at her real dumb-like. She, of course, ignored him vehemently. She was mad at him. What didn't he understand? Thinks she's just a little girl? Well, she'd show him, she thought defiantly.

Dannah vowed not to tell Cole about the cave she'd found. If he didn't want to talk to her, fine—she didn't need him. She'd explore it herself. She didn't need anyone. She would finally succumb to throwing a poignant glare at him, remembering the cruel words he had said to her at the falls the week before. Ain't no baby, that'll teach him, she thought.

She could feel him watching her again. Not like before —not with a smirk, not with some half-whispered joke waiting on his lips. Just staring. Heavy and quiet, like he was trying to figure something out. She ignored him, ignored the heat that crept up her neck.

Cole quickly turned back to Preacher Menard's sermon, pretending to care. How could he have been so cruel to push Dannah away so suddenly? Why had he done that? She was his best friend, but he couldn't talk to her the way he once had.

Dannah grew more and more content on her decision to keep the cavern a secret. Why was he at the falls, anyway? Seemed all he'd done lately was go out of his way to not talk to her and watch her. No time for hunting, no time for swimming. "Stupid Cole," she muttered.

Dannah whispered to her sister sitting next to her and carefully concealed her pointed finger. "Elisabeth, look." Mr. Wilkinson had made the fatal mistake of falling asleep next to Billy Edwards. Billy had successfully balanced the good book on the edge of Ned Wilkinson's knee. It would only be a matter of time.

And sure enough, when his snoring was getting increasingly louder not two minutes later, his wife nudged him awake. The Bible fell to the ground with a loud *thwap* and caught more than just the sisters' attentions.

But worse still, when Mr. Wilkinson jolted awake from the smack of the book, he also let go of an angry grunt, hitting his wife in the face with his flailing arms. Preacher Menard peered over his tiny half-spectacles, cleared his throat, and continued.

Dannah was always out of her church dress and out

the cabin door before Pa had even unhitched the horses. Past the northern line of trees and into the hills that ran east of the river, she managed to find her new place again. It was a grand cave, all her own.

Caverns were scattered all about the Hill Country, a few complete with drawings and everything. Pa said Indian drawings used to decorate people's homes. The dwellings were dug into the hillside that backed to the river.

She had explored them on lazy Sundays just as this one. She quickly learned to be careful in the summer when most of the caves were inhabited by an enormous number of bats. She was scared and amazed by them. She had touched a dead one once. It felt like velvet along her fingertips. A couple dozen expeditions had left Cole and Dannah with more than a mason jar full of flint and other treasures.

Dannah found an arrowhead shard near the entrance to her new cave and was certain there would be more inside. The opening was almost completely covered in growth. She cut through a section just big enough to crawl through without giving away her refuge to any critters.

As soon as she was up on her feet again and not but a couple steps inside, she learned the ground was not firm. The rocks slid down and gave way underneath her feet. It kept going, too. It was a good foot before Dannah's ankle found solid ground and then the rest of her atop the ankle.

"Damn it!" her yell echoed. The chamber must have

opened up further inside for such a loud echo to return. She heard her own moans come back from the close walls. She attempted to stand after a while of rubbing her ankle and soothing her ego. When that did not work, she reluctantly crawled toward her pack and the entrance.

The search would have to continue another day, and she was certain that it would be a good one. Dannah made her way ever so slowly to the riverbank using a shotgun as a cane. She knew he was there instantly.

She would have recognized that confounded whistling anywhere, but she was certainly not going out of her way to avoid him. She couldn't really; it took her a half hour to come this far.

So she continued past a mounted Cole, only fifty feet away now. She didn't look up at him, but the clicking of the barrel against the ground gave her tiptoeing away.

"What the hell happened to you?" He froze, watching her pass with a determined scowl upon her face.

"What do you want, Cole?" She rocked back on her left heel and sprang forward in an effort to pick up her stuttered momentum.

"Well? What happened?" He lifted himself off Samuel and into a little run.

"Nuthin'."

"Well, something made you bleed like that."

"Just a clumsy little girl, I guess." Dannah mumbled. Cole looked from her face to her loaded crutch and back again, remorseful for having angered her so badly. He should have known better. Dannah didn't anger at him easily, but when she did, it was, to say the least, regrettable. He hadn't meant to take anything out on her; she was his best friend. He just felt so confused these days, especially when he was around her.

"Always were handy with that shotgun. Sit down right here." He ignored her insolence and grabbed her elbow, throwing her off balance. He sat her atop a flat rock and laid the gun on the ground just out of her reach.

He tried to get Dannah's boot off, but the pressure from the top of the boot pulled on her ankle and she kicked her leg in defense, nearly striking him in the face. Cole swiftly dodged her kick but fell on the ground, catching himself just before he rolled backward into the river.

"Stop that! Drat, that hurts…" Dannah shut herself up by biting the inside of her bottom lip. She just couldn't stand to hear him call her a baby again.

After recovering, Cole stood again at her feet and placed his hands on her boot but stopped, shook his head in self-protest, "One of us bleeding is enough. Let's try something else." He moved to her side and picked her up in his arms before she could argue. He backed up into the water, waist-high in the river and almost completely covering Dannah's shoulders.

"What the hell do you think you're doing?" Dannah wiped water out of her eyes.

"Don't get your back up! We're just going to let your boot fill up with water, and it should slide right off. You may not even kick me."

"Sorry," Dannah gave a tiny, telling smile. She couldn't help but close her eyes as Cole rocked her back and forth in the water. She fought the urge to close her eyes by biting down on her lip again. His arms felt like the comfort of a warm bed, the water like sinking into a deep sleep. She tried again to resist the heaviness of her lids, like she was lying awake, on watch for midnight marauders. But they gave way to the comfort of his arms as he shifted her closer into his chest.

Cole kept his movements steady, his arms firm but careful around her. The water lapped against them, warm where the sun touched, cool in the deeper pockets of the river. He swallowed hard, trying to ignore the way she felt against him—softer than he expected.

She let her head tilt, eyes slipping closed, her breath evening out against his. His grip on her tightened, just for a second. Too long. He forced himself to focus on the water, on the task. Nothing else.

He finally felt her muscles relax, but he became more and more tense and aware of his surroundings and their closeness. "I think that should do it." He was on the shore again, and the boot was off without even a yelp from her.

"I don't think the ankle's broken. Scraped up your leg pretty good though." He turned her leg to examine it, careful to let her heel rest on the ground.

"You know, we could have just dipped my foot in the water?"

"Could have. But would you have listened?" He grinned at her as he walked off. "I'll be right back."

Dannah hurriedly wrung out the corners of her shirt and pants and patted them down as best she could without disrobing.

"This will sting a little," he said, walking up from behind her. He put some burdock leaves on her ankle and wrapped it up with the damp shirt that he had stripped off. He slowly patted more burdock on the scratches that ran up her calf, and then he quickly rolled down her pant leg.

"Good as new. So you gonna tell me what were you doing?" Cole said, looking up from her leg.

"Nope. First, you gonna tell me why you said such mean things to me?" She raised one eyebrow at him. He gazed upon her for a long moment and then burst into an abrupt laugh.

"Why are you laughing at me?" She hit her fist down against the big rock she was resting on.

"I'm not laughing at you. I just forgot that about you."

"Forgotten what?" Dannah said with her knuckles now turning white.

"No matter what is on your mind. You sure don't hold anything back when something is bothering you." He was too close. Close enough that she could see the gold flecks in his eyes, the way his throat bobbed when he swallowed.

"Never figured I had to 'round you. Never thought you kept anything from me nei—"

His mouth found hers and pressed against it softly, like a question at first. His warmth rushed through her like a flood. Like her wound had opened up deeper, she was overcome with rushing tenderness. Like something long overdue, something neither of them could take back.

He pulled her in close by the elbows, but their lips never parted. They only softened enough to steal short, shallow breaths from each other.

CHAPTER FIFTEEN

The sun was setting as Dannah made her way home from hay cutting. Elisabeth would be worried. She had told her sister that she would be back hours ago. Dannah felt better; the fever was sweated away from the hours in the field. Doc was wrong. It was the work that made her feel better, grow stronger. It was her time left vacant to think that sent her deeper into her mattress. She was hungry, though, and she hoped Elisabeth would have replaced what she had dropped on the floor by now.

In the distance, Dannah could see the cabin door was open. Dannah came upon Queen Esther frantically digging at the chicken coop wall. "Queeny, stop that! Where's Elisabeth?"

Dannah ran up the porch steps with one single bound and inside the cabin. Her stomach clenched as she swung the door further open, banging softly against the frame in the wind. Her breath caught. Inside, chairs lay toppled, the bench overturned. The bedchamber door gaped open, a hollow mouth in the dim light. Empty.

"Elisabeth!" Her voice broke as she lunged for the bedroom, already knowing she wouldn't find her.

Neither Ma nor Lizzie was anywhere to be seen. Dannah didn't hesitate. She jumped on Daisy and started off hard toward town, spotting two sets of fresh wagon tracks, one in and one out of the ranch.

She knew exactly where to go. Dannah knew they'd come back for her. That son of a bitch Hillard's been doing Henry Edwards' dirty work again, she thought. He had been the rider that day. The very hand that held her atop the horse. She could still feel his grasp at her back.

Sheriff Hillard had dragged her mother down a mile of river that day. Dannah could only imagine her ma didn't give him quite the good fight this time around. He had finally come back to finish the job, no doubt as Edwards' lackey.

Hillard was a puppet. He was no saint, but he was stupid. Mama hardly had the strength to sit up in bed; there was no fight in her. Plucked out of the very bed that had been her resting place since the dragging. That bed must have haunted her, just as she haunted the cabin for Dannah.

Actually, as Elisabeth had pointed out many times before, she was more dead before the dragging happened. Physically now she was gone, but that spark in her eyes of being present had not been there before the dragging.

Just before her father left, there were nights that Dannah lay awake and listened to the creak… creak… of her mother's rocking chair. The chair had been fashioned from an old wagon wheel and a barrel that stored salted meats on their journey to Medea, back when Daniel and Clare had forged into the wilderness, hand in hand.

It made that long, dragging sound—like a wagon rolling over rock.

She just sat facing her and Daniel's bedroom. The door would be closed with him inside, but it didn't matter to her; she just watched it.

Dannah'd pass her on the way to the outhouse, without a word between them. Those were the good nights, when there was no pretending. No attempt to conceal the devastation she felt from her husband. Only the chair spoke then, creaking low and steady. He had changed so dramatically and practically overnight, too. Mama just couldn't catch up.

At first, it was yelling from their bedroom, but it couldn't be contained. It swelled like dough, to slamming doors and smashing chairs and crying, wretched crying.

Dannah couldn't handle her pa smashing things and yelling, and she certainly couldn't handle her mama's crying. Eventually, Pa would shut the door and shut Clare's whimpering out of their bedroom. "What have I done?" Ma rocked and nodded over and over at the closed door. It never answered though, or maybe it did, and Dannah just couldn't hear as she could. That sound of the rocking filled the whole room. It got inside her. It stayed.

Men wield silence like a weapon. Women sink into it like African quicksand. Those were the hard nights, where Elisabeth and Dannah found each other once again, lying close together up in the loft.

Even up there, they could still hear it. That creak, like a rope pulling tighter. After their father left for good, Ma didn't cry anymore; she just went empty.

It was haunting but far more bearable. Dannah worked, Elisabeth sobbed, Mama rocked. They knew Daniel was with Mattie Edwards; everyone did. By that time the whole town was talking about it and how Henry Edwards was being made a fool by that Yankee woman of his. Somehow, they'd all forgotten Henry was a carpet-bagger himself, and the Marshall women were entirely forgotten in the midst of the gossip.

Ma told the girls he had gone to San Antone with the new wrangler to see about replenishing the remuda, but he'd already been gone for a week at that point. It took her that long to find the words for a lie, and she didn't find many for Dannah after that. Just rocking and pacing about the house as a ghost would have done.

At first, she had supper ready when Dannah'd come in from the field. But long weeks of pacing and waiting, and pulling at her hair, and every day she seemed a little further away.

Not long after, Queen Esther even stopped paying attention to her when she walked past. This grew into the dog carefully circling far around her, like Ma and that old rocking chair were vexed. It groaned beneath her, like it knew it had become the only thing keeping her tethered. Elisabeth said animals could sense a person's soul. Ma's soul must have been gone.

She didn't ask questions; she didn't respond to Dannah most of the time; she didn't look up or away from her hands resting upwards upon her lap. And she never stopped rocking. Dannah took over more and more of Ma's housework, as did Elisabeth, but she could only do so much as she tired very easily. Some days, they just didn't eat.

They all went forward in silence with only the sounds of the cabin to disrupt it: the berries trickling against the roof, the belch of the stove, the swelling gulp of the logs in the hot summer wind. And beneath it all, always, the creaking. A metronome to grief.

At night, Dannah fell more and more awake as she lay in bed. She just lay there restless, thinking most nights, turning over and over again. Thinking about the long-horn, hiring on a wrangler, finally finishing the corral, or preparing food. Her list marched through her head like a town parade. Hearing the creak of the cabin settling. The sound of the wind sneaking through the gaps in the logs. Dannah would get up to chop wood in hopes of cutting through her thoughts and her anger at Pa for leaving her to it all.

Then the night came when she didn't hear the cabin door open. She must have just shut that memory down; Dannah couldn't recall where she was exactly. She didn't hear Queeny stir, and she didn't hear his footsteps.

But she did hear Elisabeth's screams, those Dannah would forever hear. When she ran in, it was too late; her father was on top of her. And Elisabeth was crying out, like she was being stabbed.

Amazingly, Clare had heard Daniel arrive. She had spent three months listening for his return, and she was ready. The gunshot rang out over Elisabeth's cries.

Mama was there to roll him off of her daughter, too. She had her wrapped up inside her arms and encircled in her legs before he even hit the ground. Clare didn't look at him.

There she was rocking again, but this time with her daughter wrapped up in her lap. Whispering something too low to hear, too soft to be meant for anyone but her. The gun lay forgotten beside them. Clare never once looked at it either.

Clare was still rocking atop the bed, soothing her child's tears when they came for her, as if her body had become the chair, the creak echoing in her bones. Dannah just stood there.

CHAPTER SIXTEEN

$\mathcal{A}$s Dannah approached the jailhouse, she braced her rifle under her arm and took aim as she kicked open the door with one hard thrust, the wood splintering against the frame.

Inside, she found the Sheriff, Henry, Billy, and Robert King sitting around a table playing poker. Hillard jumped to his feet and reached for his pistol, but Dannah shot in his general direction.

The Edwards men kept on playing their hands. Henry Edward, with his feet propped on a barrel, didn't even look up.

"No need to start being a gentleman now, Sheriff. Sit." Dannah motioned him down with her gun.

"Well," Billy muttered, flicking his cigarette into a tin. "If it ain't the queen of Medea."

"Where the hell's my mother?" She looked directly at Henry Edwards.

"Put your gun down, Miss Dannah. Unless you want trouble, then fly." Hillard said, with one hand raised in the air, the other sliding down to his holster. His body was slightly twisted away from her. Doc Olsen came into the room from the interior hallway. He didn't look directly at Dannah either.

"I want my mother, now," Dannah cocked the rifle. "I know it was you Edwards." She motioned for Hillard to put both hands up.

"Dannah." The Doc wiped his hands clean with a handkerchief. "Sweetheart, she's gone." He said, stepping between her and the Sheriff.

She let another shot ring toward the ceiling as if she herself was letting go of a pained howl. It wasn't intended to be a warning shot, but she just couldn't decide who to kill first.

"She's inside if you'd like to see her. Her heart finally just gave out." Doc reluctantly looked up at her and tucked his handkerchief away.

"At last, you got her, you son of a bitch. What did you do to her?" Dannah raged as she looked at Edwards, taking a long, slow sip of whiskey. He even gave it an audible slurping sound as if to spite her.

Billy was on his feet, an open whiskey bottle in his hand and outstretched toward her. "Dannah," he mouthed quite condescendingly, "The Lord only gives us a certain amount of time on this here earth."

Doc Olsen took another step between Dannah's gun

and the men again. "Let's say goodbye to your mother, Dannah." He motioned toward the hallway.

"And my sister?" She burst out, not budging. At this even Henry Edwards stopped his sipping and shuffling to look up at her. "What have you done with Elisabeth?" She demanded.

Billy stood arrogantly with his leg propped up on the chair, his elbow crossed over his thigh. He swung the whiskey bottle back and forth, dangling it from his fingertips.

"Answer me!" She yelled as she let another shot ring out. The bullet hit his bottle, and it exploded into a million pieces. Billy fell back, bringing the chair with him to the floor. His foot slid forward, jamming in-between the wooden slats of the chair.

Dannah leisurely reloaded the rifle in the midst of the chaos. When Billy finished fondling at his chest and realized he wasn't shot, he hurled the remaining shard of bottleneck that he had been left holding. Yelling, "Crazy bitch!" over and over into the quiet void that the boom had created in the room. She followed Doc into the hallway.

Doc led her back into a damp cell. Dannah only took one step inside. She looked down at her mother, wrapped up in the horse blanket they plucked from her very own stables.

"Don't worry, dear, I will get her back home for you." She nodded at the Doc and took the step backwards out of the cell. She left the jailhouse without a word.

Outside, the heat pressed against her skin, suffocating. The wind kicked up dust around her boots, and for a second, she swayed on her feet, her hands still locked too tight around the gun. Maybe Elisabeth had been hiding in the coop or the root cellar.

CHAPTER SEVENTEEN

She rode fast and stayed on the banks of the river as much as possible. The rain had started up again today. And it was much easier to maneuver on the narrow clay banks than the spongy trail.

She passed the burrow Queeny's digging had created at the coop wall, which was now pooling. The fire was on inside, and she breathed a sigh of relief as she passed through the doorway.

"Elisabeth where were you?" she called out.

"I've been here." She came out from the stove and shut the cabin door behind Dannah to stop the wind from bringing in more rain.

"Elisabeth," Dannah stood in her path back into the kitchen, "She's gone! They've killed her, Lizzie." Her chest heaved.

"I know. Don't take on so." She looked up from a

mixture of batter and let the bowl come to a rest on her hip. "She was ready for them this time, Dan."

"What do you mean? Did you give her a gun?"

"No, not ready like that. I mean it was time. Said it was time for us to let go of her," she said, stirring again.

"Not like this. Not by their bloody hands." Dannah shook her head violently.

"Dannah, it doesn't matter the means, this time she was ready and awaiting her fate."

"How? What happened here?" Dannah straightened up and looked around the room confused, as if she were missing a vital piece of the puzzle.

"Don't you see? They came here in the name of justice." Elisabeth didn't look back up at her sister.

"No! They came here to fake vengeance and for greed." Dannah protested.

"Upon which they will be judged, not her, and that is our justice, Dannah." The scrape of the spoon in the bowl swished around again.

"What about hers? Her justice?"

"Hers is in knowing her daughter will be watched over by her spirit and freed from her living ghost and her burden. Her sins, not yours Dannah!" An awkward silence fell between the girls. "She wasn't getting better." Elisabeth's eyes widened, and her voice got very steady. "She was holding on for you. You two are the same kind of stubborn. You can never let go of anything. Always have been that way. Let go of her."

"Let go? Of what? Of her murder? She's not even in the

ground!" Dannah grabbed her sister's arms so she'd stop mixing the damn batter. "What is wrong with you?"

She gave Elisabeth a violent shake at the shoulders, her whole body swung about. She finally set the bowl down on the wooden preparing table. "You remember when I got the yellow fever. Mother and Father didn't leave my side for weeks. But you stopped talking to me completely. Why did you do that?"

Dannah took a small step back and replied out of the side of her mouth, "I don't know. I guess I was mad at you for getting sick."

"You called me a yellow-bellied fever-faker."

Dannah let go of a bit of a smirk. "Well, you did used to pretend to be sick a lot to get out of school."

"I burned hot with fever for three weeks!" Elisabeth said with a tiny burst of laughter.

"I know it was stupid. I was just angry and scared of losing you, I guess. I don't really remember." Dannah tried to concentrate on Elisabeth, but she couldn't help but look around the room.

Elisabeth finally looked at her. "Ma was bigger than you, too."

"You remember when Father had to borrow money against the ranch to bring medicines in from the Galveston shore. I begged him not to, I told him I'd fight it, I swore I'd get better. But when I heard Ma and Pa talking with Mr. Edwards about selling some of our land, first my heart broke from the weight that rested on my back, but then, well, after a while I had to let it go. It was just too much to bear. I couldn't stop them. Dannah, you can't always control what happens and you can't always control others. Your fate lies in not only what God has written for You, but also for what He's written for whatever Us you are a part of. We will bury our mother and lay dirt on the part of Us we lost today. And we will pray."

Elisabeth walked to the table, picked up the bowl again and commenced her scraping and stirring. As if her hands had never stopped moving at all.

Dannah watched her in silence. The scrape of the spoon against the wood filled the cabin, rhythmic and endless.

CHAPTER EIGHTEEN

Mama was laid to her final rest on the hilltop that she used to stand watch on for Daniel and Hannah to come in from the herd. The very one they all used to picnic upon. Ma and her Hannah used to lay foot to foot at the crest and set themselves sailing down the hill, till they reached the bottom reeling. She'd spend an hour picking grass out of her daughter's hair and Sunday dress, giggling. Only to climb to the top and roll down it just once more, which of course became several more times before the day was done.

Preacher Menard continued his monotone eulogy for the sparse cluster of mourners and ranch hands that gathered. There were the bastards, Sheriff Hillard and Henry Edwards, neighborly Mr. Hartwell, Rufus and his crew, and a handful of obligated neighbors or interested buyers.

"Go to the river, Brothers and Sisters. That old river, those old ways... "

Their soft, unmelodious singing was carried with the wind away from the hill and down into the crevices of the valley below.

Dannah didn't stand among them. Couldn't.

Instead, she perched high in the branches of an old oak, the same way she had when she was a girl hiding from trouble. Only this time, there was no trouble—just a grave, and a mother she couldn't bring herself to bury.

Below, Elisabeth stood still as stone, lost beneath the weight of their mother's bonnet and black dress. She never turned, never looked for Dannah. She knew better. Dannah wasn't part of this. Not anymore. Her head bowed, straightened shoulders, and hands taut to her side the whole time. Elisabeth never even mentioned the funeral to Dannah afterward. It's like she wasn't there, but she always had a way of staying invisible to everyone but Dannah.

She must have known Dannah couldn't stand amongst them and mourn their mother. Even she, herself, had to separate. She stood ghostly still, a good ten feet outside the tiny half circle of mourners.

They began to scatter as the service came to an end, and with an "Amen I say to you" from Preacher Menard, they slowly disappeared. Elisabeth vanished among them, too.

All that remained was the freshly turned ground, and a small mound of flowers placed upon her. It looked so strange bulging forth in the grassy pasture.

A short while after the gathering cleared, Dannah

climbed down from her branch. She couldn't concentrate long enough to think, let alone pray. She reached the ground in time to see a figure approaching the gravesite, picking up the flowers that the light rain had pushed away. It was Cole. He gently placed them back at the foot of the mound. Dannah decided to head for her work in the opposite direction.

Cole knew she was there; he could feel her presence. He turned his head to see a lean shape walking down the hillside; he just knew it was her. But Cole wasn't there for Dannah, so he turned his back to her to grieve for himself.

Mrs. Marshall had been around more than his own mother growing up. She used to patch up the scrapes he had collected on the little excursions Dannah and him frequently took.

One time they were fishing, and Cole pierced himself through the inner elbow with a hook. He was so embarrassed when Dannah came home with a basket full of perch and there Cole was with a bloodied hook stuck in his arm. The confounded bait was still attached and all.

"Cole, darling, if you wanted to catch something bigger, you'd be better off using minnows. Those fish will never believe in a worm this big," she had said, removing the hook gently from his arm. She smiled ferociously into his eyes and stroked the side of his head tenderly.

He should have told Mrs. Marshall what he had seen, Cole thought. Maybe she could have washed her hands of her husband sooner. Maybe things would have been different. Instead, he chose to confide in Billy. Why? He asked himself so many times.

He knew Billy never could keep a secret, and the last person who needed to know was his father. But the sight of his own mother and Daniel Marshall in the act had set his mind on fire. He just didn't know what to do with it.

After all, he was still quite confused with what had happened with Doris on his birthday. He had so many questions and guilty feelings about it. After that encounter, Cole found that carving was one of the only things that didn't leave him with room for thought.

All he intended to do was to go to The Grand Hotel to give his mother the cardinal that he had made special for her. It took him two weeks to get it just right. Started working on a golden cheek warbler but couldn't figure out the yellow striping. Once he settled on the cardinal, he couldn't find a wood that pleased him. Finally, he chose oak. And after weeks of work, it was perfect, down to the loose feather on its tail. He took another whole week to dress it up just right. He even let it soak in berry juice to stain it the right color. It was her birthday; it had to be perfect.

Cole's mind came back to Mrs. Marshall's grave for just a moment and then back to The Grand Hotel. He remembered bolting up the hotel's staircase and bursting open the door. He thought for sure they had seen him. But he must not have been as loud as he imagined.

He stood there in the hallway and called for her, but it must have been just a whisper, because it was soon obvious neither his mother nor Mr. Marshall knew he was there. He never did give his mother the cardinal. He threw it in the river and watched it float away.

He didn't speak to anyone for weeks, besides the occasional nod and a couple of "yes sirs". He just went inside his own head, retreating into the shallow comforts of work. It was his sole distraction in trying to shake the incident. He vomited at least once a day for the first week, but he attributed that to the intense heat that had settled in early. His father had been right; he was a man now, no time for playing around.

Until one day, Cole lost it. The fact that he had let it slip to his brother Billy, he'd never forgive himself for that. It welled up in him like a twisting fist inside his stomach, and Billy kept balking about Mother coming home, said she was feeling better. He didn't see it coming; Cole just snapped.

He went in to give Billy a wallop, but instead he yelled at him. He yelled so loud that Billy squinted. He yelled and spat the words out until Billy knew the whole ordeal. Like he was delivering a blow to him more painful than any punch could bring, although his fists stayed clenched up the whole time. And when he was done, he saw his brother shrink up the same way he had.

An hour later, when his father returned home, Billy had stopped crying and told his father everything. Apparently, Billy didn't have the stomach for the ordeal either. But it was like Henry didn't hear him. Cole sat behind the door silently listening to Billy spew all the details at his father. He even made up some raunchier ones, as if he were describing what he had seen in his own mind, not what Cole had told him.

After Billy had finished, their father left the cabin and did not return that night. It was never spoken of again. Maybe a week went by, and then Mattie got real sick again, and the idle talk of Mother coming home ceased altogether. The doctors said they were baffled; it was "just supposed to be an Indian disease," they said, padding the news for Henry Edwards' sake. Not once did they acknowledge the truth. She had contracted a whore's disease.

Sometime after that, Cole learned to let that day slip from his waking memories, like it had his father's. Cole did often wonder how long it took his father to erase it. He wondered when the first day was that it didn't sneak into the back of his father's eyeballs. Cole hadn't had that day yet.

CHAPTER NINETEEN

By the time Dannah stepped inside the cabin, the funeral already felt like something that had happened to someone else.

The air was thick, humid with the lingering rain, and her dress clung to the back of her neck. She wanted to lie down. Wanted to forget. But then she saw the letter, half-crumbled where it had fallen from her hat. She had received expedited post from her Grandfather John in Austin, but now it lay there, waiting.

She now made a habit of tucking her post away, in hopes of preventing anyone from spreading her business around town. Besides the doggone Postmaster, that is, she knew that was futile.

With a sigh, she sat down on the oak chest, her body heavier than it should have been.

. . .

MY DEAREST CHILD,

Many deep regrets that I cannot join you to grieve for your mother. Clare, my beautiful daughter, will be missed beyond the telling of it.

It seems the torrential rain that Austin is incurring makes the trip impossible. I had held out hope that the skies might clear in time. But the season is against us until the summer arrives, which is sure to be soon enough. The damp aggravates my rheumatism terribly, and the mosquitoes seem determined to finish what age has begun. Forgive the complaint; it is only that I feel the sting of impotence keenly.

I wish I could have given my sweet daughter my heart when hers gave out. I have no use for mine now. The Lord plays cruel games to have to endure outliving two children. There is no word for such grief, only the slow work of learning to bear it.

Oddly, the rain brings cheer to others here. The newspapers speak of it as a blessing: fields restored, rivers swelled, and prospects improved. They claim it may revive interest in that much-debated railroad expansion. The politicians are drunk on speculation, and I find myself something of an unwilling expert now, having endured the prattle.

I know far too much about those Chinamen camps that have built up the northern tracks. This is all thanks to a terribly dull gathering I attended last month at the acclaimed Driskill Hotel. When it comes to politics, I am at sea, my dear. They say it should bring more people out here and most likely your way, too. There is much excitement over the bounty of Boerne and Kerrville that lie near the rail.

The future is upon us, they say. Strange how the future

never seems to arrive for those of us buried in the past. Forgive my wandering pen. It is the mind's way of reaching toward you.

Aunt Mari and your cousins send their deepest condolences. They speak often of you and would welcome your presence here, should you wish to try your hand at life in the Capitol. There are many young men here of excellent mind and ambition— perhaps not unlike your grandfather in younger days. I suspect your mother would approve such a future, though I leave that thought with gentle humility.

Do write when you are able. And give my kindest regards to your father.

Yours Most Affectionately,

Grandfather John

Dannah tucked the letter deep into the bottom of her trunk, buried under the church shoes she never wore. She, of course, would not be writing back and felt no obligation to tell him the status of her father.

Let him sit in his fine house, in his city full of flush young men and men who knew nothing of blood in the dirt. He wanted to send regards to her father? Let him find the bastard himself. Some things were best left buried and some unanswered.

Late that night, after everyone had gone to bed, Cole came through their darkened door easily and stepped over Queeny without detection. It felt like such a long time since he had been in that cabin. He had forgotten that Mr. Marshall had added a bedroom onto the back of the cabin and the loft where the girls used to stay had been converted into supply space. It still smelled the same though, slightly sweetened.

He nudged Dannah's shoulder ever-so carefully and then stroked the part of her arm exposed from the blankets.

"Dannah," he crouched beside her at an arm's-length distance, fairly safe he thought. He had experienced Dannah's response to having a surprise visit twice this month. Once he had been threatened with her gun, and the other had left him with mysterious bite marks that still had not healed. Seeing her asleep though, he couldn't help but put his guard down.

The touch was light—barely there, like the whisper of a dream. Warm fingertips traced along her cheekbone, brushing down to the curve of her chin. Dannah exhaled softly, sinking deeper into the haze of sleep.

"I thought you were supposed to be knee-deep in San Saba grass without me," she murmured, her voice slipping out before she was fully awake.

Now he was doing the smiling, and he ran the back of his fanned fingertips across her chin and mouth and closed his eyes tight. She was thinking about them once upon a time, his last trip to Llano to be exact. She had snuck out to the river in the middle of the night to wish him a safe trip before he left in the morning. The trip was with his father to secure some more breeding stock.

They had already seen each other in the afternoon. But he wanted to sip her in at the very last moment, so he could make it last that much longer, as if he were holding his breath. In a way, Cole figured they were holding their breath that entire summer, not just during their time apart. That summer they had shared a snippet of happiness that neither of them wanted to end. It was just like yesterday to him, when a few days apart from one another felt like saying goodbye forever. He tried his hardest not to reminisce, but it was satisfying to hear that Dannah floated back there too, despite her best efforts.

"Dannah, wake up. I have to show you something." In an instant, she snatched up his hand at the wrist and gave it a sudden twist counterclockwise. Before she had her eyes fully open, she had him on his side pleading, "Woman, trust me, it's real important."

"I'm not goin' anywhere with a four-flusher. You're crazy. And lucky I don't shoot you for breaking into my home."

"Dannah," he came up on his knees again, eye level on the bed and surrendered his hand to her pressure, "Trust me, you want to see this." She realized she was still twisting his hand, but he had the leverage to begin twisting back so they were just holding hands now. And the cunning boy gave her a gentle, reassuring squeeze. Dannah quickly let go.

He recovered his hand and left the room. She heard him go out the front door. He knew she'd come after him, no better bait than curiosity. She tucked her nightgown into her skirt as she quietly stepped over Queeny, who was still soundly sleeping. She shook her head in amazement, grabbed her gun, and was out the door.

He didn't say a word to her. She followed him bareback on Daisy. She knew at this hour of the morning they wouldn't be seen together, so she rode fairly close. She hated feeling like she was blindly following Cole into the woods any longer; she had grown too wise for those days.

After a while had passed, he brought Samuel down to a walking pace and jumped off him just on the outside of town. She shot Cole a threatening look as they tied the horses to a tree, and he signaled for her to follow toward the livery stable with his finger over his lips. He didn't stop till they were wedged between the drugstore and Russell Payne's place. Dannah hesitantly took her cues from Cole as they ducked behind a couple of oak barrels. Finally, Cole looked Dannah square in the eyes. "Are you ready?"

"For?" She twanged out as unimpressed as she could muster. It was obvious that her curiosity had surged with the silent ride into town. What on earth could have made Cole Edwards bold enough to dare break into her cabin, she wondered? Did he realize how close she came to killing his kin just days before in the jailhouse?

"For? The funniest damn thing you've ever seen!" He proceeded to point to the center of the square, spinning his finger toward the sky and whistling in a soft, whirly manner.

She followed his finger up, up, up … to the most amazing sight she could have imagined. It took her a very slow minute to put it together in the dark. But there it was. Her eyes widened with recognition as she made out the shape of Sheriff Hillard hanging from a rope strung from the top of the jailhouse and clear off the roof, his legs limp and dangling in mid-air. The rope was tied around his waist and ran up into the air to an unknown anchor. He was buck naked, and it didn't take long for Dannah to ascertain that he was most certainly soaked drunk. Apparently, he had gone out of his mind and out of his drawers, Dannah thought.

His lack of sobriety became increasingly obvious. His legs began running in circling motions. Dannah just watched with a gaping mouth. Every few seconds his legs would cease from their rapid cycling, and he'd sweep his arms in broad windmill-like jerking movements side to side, causing his whole body to twist in dizzy spins back to center. Dannah thought it looked like a crazy tribal dance.

His contortions finally stopped when he somehow managed to turn himself ass-side up against the rope. He struggled in staggered intervals, using the line to pull himself up without so much as a grunt. Must have been sober enough to know he'd never live down the sight of his bare moonlit ass flailing over his own jailhouse. He kept pretty quiet and continued to struggle for freedom. At one point, he got himself about three feet up the rope using his thighs to pull up, before giving up. His arms seemed to be of no help at all to the battle. He did let a yelp go when he slid back down the rope.

Dannah finally looked over at Cole. He had just been watching her, enjoying her utter amazement. He had his arms crossed in contentment, and he leaned back against a barrel, all grins. He acted like he had brought her a wonderful gift, like Queeny brings back rats.

Cole stood back; arms crossed. He rocked on his heels, waiting—watching Dannah's face shift from confusion to stunned delight.

"Well?" he finally drawled. "Ain't he a sight?"

He looked downright pleased with himself, and for a second, Dannah almost laughed at the absurdity of it all.

Cole let his teeth show through his widening lips and

topped it off by displaying a deep dimple on his left cheek. "How—did you? Did you do this?" she asked.

At first, Cole was stunned that Dannah thought this could be his own handiwork, but he was also torn about taking credit because of her obvious amazement. He kept silent.

Their attention came back to Hillard when he began vomiting. He pulled back on the rope and tried to shimmy the noose up to his chest in order to loosen the weight against his stomach. He must have passed out from exertion because his legs finally came to rest. But they weren't sticking around to find out, as a couple of lanterns lit up in the hotel.

Dannah couldn't control herself. She threw her head back in satisfied laughter as they headed back to Daisy and Samuel. She nearly broke into a sideways gallop.

"No, I didn't by the way. But I think I know who did." Cole finally came clean when they reached the horses, before Dannah had a chance to ask again.

"Who then?"

"Two Mexicans Hillard arrested today, I think. I saw him bring them in this afternoon. Then when I saw them pass with some others on the trail tonight, I figured something must be wrong. The Sheriff had said they were caught horse thieving and to keep an eye out for more stragglers. He didn't think they were working alone. I mean they were damn lucky to be brought in breathing with no branches tied to their corpses, but to be set free, I figure that ain't possible. I came out the saloon, pretty late and I usually cut through between the saloon and the line, like everyone else to avoid the jailhouse, but tonight, I went through town. When I spotted him hanging there he was completely passed out, he must be sobering up now. Made for a good show huh?" Cole was laughing again with Queeny's familiar approval-seeking expression.

"Thank you," Dannah ceased her smiling and gave Cole a nod as she mounted Daisy. "Better be getting back now," and she was on her way before Cole even had a chance to untie Samuel.

His neck instantly began to spasm. It took only a moment for him to register the look on her face. Cole struggled to get on Samuel.

Dannah had doubled back before she hit the open patch of the trail, about five hundred feet deeper into the brush. She had only seconds before Cole caught on. But that was all she needed.

Cole rode straight into the thick trying to cut her off but found only her trail. It led him back into town just in time to see her frozen right in front of a dangling Hillard. She was still mounted, and her rifle was aimed toward the sky.

Dannah inhaled, slow and deep, the rifle steady against her shoulder. Hillard hung limp, spinning slightly in the wind. A stupid, drunk man. A cruel one. A dead one.

She exhaled, squeezed the trigger.

The shot cracked through the night. The Sheriff's body jolted, his stomach split open, and blood splattered against the jailhouse wall.

Dannah relaxed her rifle against her breast, but she kept it aimed at Hillard's body. She traced its heavy pendulum swings in the air until she was sure the Sheriff's muscles weren't moving on their own account.

Only then did she tuck the rifle beneath the blanket and ride home through the brush.

Cole didn't go after her.

It was perfect; she thought. No one would question who had shot Hillard, and those Mexicans would be halfway to San Antone before people put two and two together.

Satisfaction flooded over her like warm water; she wouldn't remember the rest of the ride home. She was undressed again and in bed, fighting off the damp air with her blanket. Dannah slept through the night for the first time since she could remember. Time had stopped for her, but she felt herself breathe in again.

Cole did not sleep.

He lay on his cot, eyes wide, staring at the ceiling as the weight of it settled in.

Hillard was dead.

Dannah had done it. She had lifted that rifle, taken her aim, and pulled the trigger without a second thought. And the worst part? She was right. The whole damn town would assume the Mexicans had done it. No one would question it.

And Cole had given her the perfect alibi.

His stomach churned. He had laughed with her, shared in her delight at the Sheriff's humiliating display

—never once thinking she would turn it into an execution.

He knew that Sheriff Hillard's blood was on his hands. He had led her straight to it. Given her the moment. Given her the means.

And now, there was no turning back. Everything happened so fast, he thought. He never fathomed Dannah would risk being condemned for murder, like her own mother had been.

CHAPTER TWENTY-ONE

*D*annah was surprised to find the stove still cold when she woke up in the morning. Elisabeth was always up before her. She had opened her eyes earlier but turned her back to the sunrise and fell again into a heavy sleep tucked in the warmth of her straw bed.

She finally went to check on Elisabeth. "Are you feeling okay? Do you need some more Hotsetter's stomach bitters?" Dannah felt Elisabeth's neck. It was ice cold.

"Just tired, I'll be up soon, I have some herbs to restock today."

"No, no you rest, I'll go. The herd will be fine till this afternoon." Dannah said, already walking out of her room. She grabbed her hat and knapsack hanging by the door. "Come on, Queeny, a little scoutin' will do you good."

Queeny was obviously up for the challenge as she was

on Dannah's heels immediately. The rain had stopped, and the winds carried the sweet, sunbaked smell of drying grass into the air.

She made her way through the woodlands, collecting some dandelions, mesquite beans, and pecans on her way to the river. Before long, she stumbled upon an abandoned hive nesting inside some exposed tree roots. The rains must have knocked it clean off its branch, and it had flooded up with water, but the honeycomb still looked capped, and it would be quite a treat.

The river was brimming. Dannah stepped across some jutting stones and made her way onto a small circular island to take inventory. Queeny stayed on shore, pacing until Dannah unwrapped some dried peaches. The sugary smell must have stuck to her wet nostrils on shore because she jumped in and paddled her way across the current to the island, nearly drowning herself in the process. When Queeny reached the island, she furiously shook dry and managed to completely drench Dannah in the process.

"You are such a beast." Dannah gave her a playful smack upon the stomach as Queeny wrestled around on her back. She found a grassy patch to dry herself upon. The wiggling and squirming seemed to thrill her into a barking frenzy, like the little land offered wild freedoms that the shoreline had kept from the old girl. Queeny proudly looked around as if she claimed the island for herself.

Dannah saw Queeny eyeing a piece of honeycomb that

was protruding from her satchel, and even the grizzly look Dannah gave didn't stop her from taking a quick lick. The two laid down, and the sun shone a warm smile down upon their tiny island. Dannah dipped her toes into the rushing water. The bright light forced her eyes shut, and the island began to rock them back and forth. It didn't take long to force them both into a sun-induced nap.

About half an hour later, Dannah was woken by an abrupt jab to her gut. The entire weight of Queeny came down on Dannah's stomach through her two front paws. She was snapping at the air in hot pursuit of a dragonfly buzzing about and obviously paying no mind to Dannah's peaceful dozing.

Her attention quickly turned to a large female map turtle that shared Dannah's idea of basking in the light. Queeny nosed at her and managed to flip the turtle on its back, revealing a triangle of dots. As Dannah rose to the turtle's rescue, she figured it was time to move on.

Their search continued rather enjoyably for the rest of the morning. They followed alongside the river's path, nestled just inside the tree line. Dannah heard the distant yelping of a hurt animal; it sounded like a calf or maybe a goat. She had to grab Queeny, the oblivious, by the tail to slow her down and listen for which direction it was coming from.

There were times Dannah suspected Queeny faked both deaf and dumb for effect, and then there were times the old girl thoroughly convinced her. She followed the crying while blocking Queeny from bolting deep into the forest. She came upon Mr. Jeffers kneeling beside one of his heifers.

"Morning, Ms. Dannah," he looked up from the cow, real sober-like. "Afraid she's gone and ran herself into the fence." Dannah knelt down beside him. "Got the screw worm. It's claimed five heads, Durhams, too, since I put that damn fence up. You'd think the dumb things would learn from example. Guess that's why we eat them and not the other way around."

He stood up, his bowed knees popping fiercely. He motioned Dannah away with the barrel of his rifle and then shot the heifer behind the ear. Queeny was startled at first by the blast and then the blood that splattered all over her face.

In just a moment, Queeny's demeanor changed from shocked to ravenous. Dannah had to stop her from lunging at the carcass. It seemed the taste for blood was indeed addictive, like Dannah suspected. Dannah pulled her back by the tail and locked Queeny firmly between her legs. So Queeny settled for licking her splattered fur and Dannah's boots.

"I'm sorry, George. How's the fence working out otherwise?"

"Well, it's our only option these days, Miss Dannah. I just caught word from Sam Lukas, that the state finished transacting the sale of ten thousand more acres for the grangers. We got to protect our plunder. They all have big plans to get rich, but it all come a cropper, if that rail don't see its way through here." He took an overdue breath.

"I suspect I have some mending to do on it now though," he looked down at the heifer. "She was a big one, did some real damage. Miss Dannah, I'm real sorry," he paused. "How are you holding up these days?"

But he didn't allow her time to answer. "Heard about your Ma. It's a damn shame, it is ... things ain't so simple as they used to be. I remember when it was just me, your daddy, and a couple other ranches out here."

He shook his head in dismay. "Them politicians sure had a way of messing with the good set-up we had going down here. We need someone to ride the river with."

Dannah peered down at Queeny, who was intensely sniffing the ground around the heifer, still bound by her knees. "State knows they got nothing to finance that rail, just our taxes and our backs."

George Jeffers was an outspoken member of the Greenback Party. He took every opportunity to preach the platform and damn both the Republicans and the Democrats. Back in '80, he'd gone door to door stumping for James B. Weaver, the Greenback man who barely scratched three percent of the vote. Still, George had been good to her family, so Dannah kept patient with his outspoken politicking.

Mr. Jeffers had stepped up for her pa at the spring roundup when Elisabeth had fallen ill with the yellow fever. He oversaw Jessie Moore, the representative that Pa had sent for the ranch. And even fired him when he started causing a ruckus at the rodeo celebration afterward.

The rodeo was always a breeding ground for trouble. It was an opportunity after the trying work of a roundup to show off cowboying skills to the surrounding ranches' hands. To drink spirits and tell trail stories of sleeping next to saddled horses, torrential thunderstorms and stupid cattle, and living off yucca after the cookie went crazy and ran off into the sunset, skillet in hand. All this was quite a common occurrence, but it never ceased to entertain.

Mr. Jeffers was still talking at her when Queeny began to wrestle with Dannah again. "Well if Janey or I can do anything for you, anything … you just come right over, you hear. I'm real sorry." He repeated again. "I know you're all alone now and my brother in Austin says your Grandpa's doin' real nice for himself at the university. Got a reputation around town for being quite…"

"Mr. Jeffers, I have to be getting home." She nodded and pulled at the Queen, who was wiggling free from her legs, for a pool of blood near the heifer.

They clumsily made off toward the river path. Queeny was salivating profusely. Drool just kept pouring from the side of her mouth, leaving a visible trail on leaves and splattering rocks in gobs as they traveled.

Seems as though even her good neighbors surmised they weren't strong enough to continue life without a man tending to them, Dannah thought. So it was unanimous; her options were to move to Austin and find a husband in one of her grandfather's society circles or move into her strange Aunt's house to raise her little brats, that is, until she birthed her own litter.

She could always marry in Medea, some disgusting old louse like Benjamin Hartwell. She was aware that her options were certainly limited with her beaming reputation, so it would have to be someone as wretched as Hartwell.

So she would let him woo her, just long enough for him to get the guts up to request the deed to her land and carry it over her feeble little head, she thought. Thus rescuing her from the rundown ranch and strapping him with a debtor's dowry, a blessed union indeed. Dannah felt sick to her stomach.

Then one day, her mind reeled further—surely she'd end up shooting him in his sleep, like the fated Hartwell himself had already warned her about. Only for her to lose the land all over again.

Or maybe she'd have bore him a bastard of a son, and he could own the ranch outright. But if she only had daughters, well, what then? Would her daughter have a better chance at holding onto their estate? "Circular solutions," she muttered.

She was nauseated and felt warm saliva pooling into the hollows of her cheeks like Queeny. Elisabeth had once accused her sister of being an Amazon. She said if Dannah could cut off her right breast, she could become a warrior with truer and steadier aim. Dannah had replied that it'd have to be both breasts, cause someone would come along wanting to suck the remaining one dry.

Too much thinking for one morning; it was making her itch. She came back to her workload. Better find some prickly pear on the way home, she thought. She was so deep in her own head, she wouldn't have noticed her own itching except for wet blood she felt under her nails. She had unknowingly scratched gouges into her arms.

CHAPTER TWENTY-TWO

Cole spent the day keeping busy in the field instead of an island. He was trying not to think about what he had brought about the night before. As the sun rose higher in the sky, Cole threw himself intensely into his work. He found it more tedious work than normal pushing the herd to the next pasture and was growing more and more angry at a defiant steer that wouldn't heed him.

He swung the lariat harder than needed, snapping it against the flank.

"Move, damn you."

The steer kicked up dirt, defiant. Cole clenched his jaw. The animal wasn't the problem. He knew that. But for a second, he needed something he could control.

He was almost out of his mind in thought and washed away in sweat when Billy found him. Billy rode up in a rush.

"Sheriff Hillard's been shot and hung!" Billy flung the words at him in a high pitch from across the field, both men on horseback. Cole thought all he was missing was a crier's hat and a bell to go with his tan duster. He didn't say anything back.

Billy continued, "Jeremiah said it was some Mexicans the Sheriff arrested yesterday." Cole exhaled deeply. "They found his keys still in the jail cell door. Bastards even stopped to drink an entire bottle of his finest whiskey, while they were stringing him up."

Cole circled back on top of one of the calves, gracefully dally roping her with his lariat. "Father said the Rangers will catch 'em," Billy continued yelling over the meowing calf. "Imagine they went south on the trail last night."

Cole slowed Samuel down. "You tell Father I saw six or so Mexicans going east through the canyon this morning. I have work left here." Cole jumped off Samuel and tended to the noosed calf, certain that Billy would relay the message to his father with his own claim on it. That was fine with Cole. The further his name was from everything, the better.

Cole had sat on the edge of his bed most of last night without realizing he had actually forgotten to lay down or undress. Well, he did remember it once, when he got up to visit the outhouse, but lost the thought to the other concerns swooping around as he returned to his spot taut to the edge of the bed. His toes touched the floor as if he were about to pounce into action.

But he felt like he was already in a sleepy dream state, replaying last night in his mind. Why had his timing with Dannah always been so off, he reveled. He shouldn't have let her ride off. She took off fast. She was setting out with a task in mind, not going home to sleep peacefully as he had imagined. He should have known.

He had seen the way she eyeballed Hillard when he led her to the scene at Payne's. He had seen her hand clenched tightly on her gun's grip at first, but he had also seen her face soften with laughter. He figured she saw the situation as he did, as amusing. Damn it, he should have reacted faster and understood her hatred for Hillard. He was always a moment behind Dannah. He closed his eyes; he felt so worn thin and stupid.

He had run upon them at the riverbanks the day of the dragging. He had seen that his father had orchestrated a mob scene.

He had seen her tossed over Hillard's steed like a blanket. One moment, her boots scraped against the earth; the next, she was airborne—gone.

Cole had locked eyes with her just before Hillard spurred the horse forward. Her mouth opened—his name ripped from her throat.

"Cole!" He would never shake the sound of her screams to him for help. Somehow, no matter how far they got down the river, her screams never seemed to fade.

He could still feel his father's grip around his bicep pulling him back. He wouldn't have even noticed Mrs.

Marshall's body bound on the ground if it weren't for the children pointing from the crowd. To this day, he wondered if Dannah had seen that his father was pointing a rifle at her. Cole knew it wouldn't have mattered to her. She would have taken a bullet in the mouth for her mother. Cole should have done the same for her, he thought.

He knew she could never understand the words his father spat through his teeth and into Cole's ear. He saw the steel barrel out of the corner of his eye and felt the weight of it come down on his shoulder. His father was using his eldest son to steady his aim at Dannah, his lover. Cole thought it was too risky to hope he'd shoot Hillard by mistake, especially with his father's flawless marksmanship.

Cole knew that his father was more than willing to jeopardize Hillard's life to get her dead. Sacrificing a lawman would be further justification for his deeds, and there would definitely be a second or third shot meant for Dannah.

His own father's piercing words rang into him, "Stay put son," he pulled him back into his own chest by the bicep, "or mark my words we'll bury two Marshall women today."

The calf bucked up, and Cole's mind came back to the hot field. He finished checking her over. Sweat poured from under Cole's hat into his eyes. He pulled his bandana up over his brow. He felt a raw blister gush open up on his hand as he ran his hand over the rope to untie the calf.

The calf didn't get up at first; she must have thought she was still bound and not realized her freedom. Cole popped her on the rear, and she struggled to her feet. When she did get steadier, she circled back dazed into the crowd calling for her mother.

Henry Edwards nursed his drink, watching the saloon in his peripheral.

Half the town was buzzing over Hillard's murder. The other half was waiting to see what Henry Edwards would do about it.

He was half-panicked and half-relieved over John Hillard's death. Henry found himself distraught over the lawlessness and brutality of the incident, right under his nose in his own damn town.

Hillard had been an asset, but a clumsy one. Hillard had failed as a lawman, but he'd be getting a new sheriff under his guidance. Sure, John was trained and loyal as hell to him, but that didn't change the fact that he was an old Confederate and a small thinker.

His death made Medea look wild, out of control. And Henry couldn't allow that—not with the rail expansion breathing down his neck.

The law was a tool, nothing more. And when a tool broke, you replaced it.

He just hoped the state would let someone of his choosing step in. They generally wouldn't have anything to say about local matters, but with the buzz of more Mississippians on their way, he knew they'd have an interest in keeping the land near the rail expansion safe for settlers and for companies.

He prayed the elections would keep them busy enough in Austin to leave him alone, just business as usual. He had big plans for little Medea County, including a gambling hall in The Grand.

After all, lots of people would be through Medea with the rail soon enough. She'd make a fine center for trading. A real cosmopolitan city, right in the belly of Texas.

He, of course, would be credited with bringing a bit of culture to the Wild West. Maybe he'd be mentioned in Buffalo Bill Cody's show as a fellow tamer. But only if Governor Hogg stayed in power. He'd seen it happen before in Kansas City. Couldn't very well let the greenbacks or Hamman get control of things. But they'd be useful enough for his cause, for the moment. He ran things uncontested until now. Before him there had been no modern conveniences, no fair trading posts, no fences, and practically no law.

But Henry Edwards knew who truly controlled the growth of Texas—the taxes, the distribution of land, and the amount of cotton being shipped overseas out of Galveston—and it wasn't the new emerging farming party, and it certainly wasn't the cattlemen anymore. They were all peons.

It was mining and big corporations; they ran the government. It was advancement and the sharing of the divine purse. He had to regain control fast; the incidents of late had sparked the state's interest too much for his liking.

CHAPTER TWENTY-THREE

Cole's body could have pushed through, but his mind couldn't hold a moment longer. He broke off and headed into the hills to find the old sod house he was born in, before the ranch house was built. He loved that soddy so much as a boy. It sat at the bottom of a tiny hill, past the Kaltenbach's sheep farm.

Along his way, he was surprised to pass another familiar site. He wouldn't have seen it had he not stopped to find his canteen. The cover had grown so thick over the cave opening, surely no one would ever find it again. It felt like another lifetime when Dannah and him had explored the cave together.

He remembered it was after her ankle healed up but before her father left. They had rekindled their friendship and their desire for spending lazy days lying on the river, fishing and exploring. It felt like an eternity ago.

They walked among the bellflowers and bluebonnets,

which grew in whites and purples and pinks. Dannah told him of her brutal days in the field alone and sleepless nights in the cabin that were made even more lonely by her mother. She had shown him her wounds from wrestling angry calves and her mishap with an iron that had left her stomach branded with a faint W and ruined one of her good work shirts. Cole gently teased her about not even getting the brand right until she showed him the scar. That hushed him up pretty quick.

Cole amazed himself when he opened up to her about his mother's sickness. Eventually they talked about the rumors that Dannah's father and her were staying at The Grand Hotel together.

Their conversation grew forced at times, but they knew they were the only ones that could possibly understand. Awkward as it was, they were more at ease after they talked. So they barreled through the versions. The rumors were never exactly the same. Cole flashed a pained smile. "Yeah, I heard Mr. Walter and Postmaster Roberson call me a 'poor child' and said Pa 'got the mitten' whatever that means."

"Ohhh!" Dannah burst out. "That must be why Mr. Walter gave me a lemon cracker!" They both chuckled on that one, as Mr. Walter was infamous for his stinginess.

"So you ever gonna tell me how you done that to yourself?" Cole said, changing the subject and pointing at her ankle.

Dannah was mindlessly inspecting the scars. "You really want to know?" Cole nodded. She gathered up her things and grabbed Cole by the hand, pulling him into the woods toward the hillside. She had forgotten all about her unfinished business at the cave earlier that summer. She marveled at that for a moment. How could such an amazing hideaway go forgotten?

With all the time she had spent these days, lying awake with her own thoughts, how had she let the new cave slip from her mind, even for a moment? She'd been too busy for child's games, she guessed.

She smiled and nodded to herself when she remembered how Cole had wounded her so badly with that very same insult not too long ago and how much it had upset her. How fast things had changed since then. Now she understood what he had meant.

"I found an arrowhead over there," She pointed and led him to the secret entrance, once again slicing at the thick vines. She tossed her pack into the opening and got on all fours. Cole followed her lead.

"Slide your feet, don't pick 'em up." They inched inside. "Ground's not too solid here."

Cole chuckled, "Ah, by all means, ladies first then."

"My pleasure," she said, always up for a challenge. She carefully stood up.

"Wait," Cole felt a stick on the ground, then pulled a matchbook and pine sap waxed cloth from his sack.

Dannah hadn't realized just how tiny the passageway was. The torch lit up the narrow pass perfectly. It was big enough for one person, and a small person at that. She was able to stand, but her hair skimmed the overhang.

Cole had to hunch over and cock his head to the side, his cheek practically resting against his chest.

She spotted a large hole where the ground had collapsed and figured that's how far her travels had previously taken her. Cole followed her lead, straddling over the hole, traveling further into the cave.

"Cole, look," She seized his wrist, extending his arm outright and aimed the flame toward the wall to reveal a colorful display. The passageway had opened up, and Cole was able to stand upright. They studied the drawings for a while, only breaking the silence with an occasional revelation.

"A bison!" Dannah ran her finger over a circle of six brown roly-poly shapes. "And horses," she continued upward, standing on her tiptoes, pulling at Cole's wrist again to light up the leaner four-legged figures.

Cole moved the torch back against the opposite wall to widen the flame's range, revealing a tiny village along the outer ring. They both let out a little gasp. "See the teepees. Must be Comanche."

"Or Coahuiltecan, they live in them, too." He ran his finger over a girl with a bronze face and black braids down her shoulder with red strung through each end.

They sidestepped along the wall, following the rolling waves of green and fish flying underneath. Neither of them realized that the tunnel had opened up into a large circular room until Cole bumped into a tiptoed Dannah, causing her to tumble sideways. She surveyed the room from her spot on the ground. Cole found a ring of stones in the center of the hollowed-out chamber, with wood still inside.

Cole lit a fire and then stabbed his torch in the ground beside Dannah. "Sorry! Are you okay?"

"Yah, this place has my blood all over it by now." She wiped her knee with her cuff. "This place needs a name, maybe it'll be more friendly if we introduce ourselves properly."

"What about Hannah's Cave? After all, you did find it."

"I think it found me. What about the Marshall-Edwards Grounds? No, I guess that sounds like a general store. Maybe it doesn't need a name. I'm sure it already has one anyway." She answered herself when Cole didn't look up at her.

"Well not for us, it doesn't! What about the Cave of the Lost Adventures?"

Dannah nodded with a smile. "That will do."

"Thank you for showing me." Cole said quickly and touched her hand. He cleared his throat upon realizing how fast the moment had turned awkward. "You hungry?" He hated feeling strange with her.

He pulled out a tin of prunes. And a couple biscuits wrapped up in a dusty blue bandana. Dannah immediately plopped down cross-legged near the fire and began chomping away.

"Thanks," she said, spitting bits of biscuit from her full cheeks.

"Here, have another," He sat down across from her and slapped his hands down on his knees. "Guess you haven't had much time for cooking lately or eating for that matter. Listen, if I can help somehow… I got things under control, and we've got some hands hired on."

Dannah was only half-listening. She had come up on her good knee and propped her weight on the opposite foot. She was desperately grabbing for another biscuit beside Cole, caddy corner from her across the fire. She had forgotten how good food felt in her mouth and that she could actually feel it filling her stomach. It had been so long; she had just grown accustomed to the wretched feeling of hunger. Something Cole did made her hesitate. Shamefully, Dannah stopped herself in mid-reach for another biscuit. She was being so awful, eating all his food like this.

Cole came up on his knees to meet her. Maybe it was the warmth of the fire or the soft glow against the cave walls, but out of nowhere he kissed her. All of her weight pressed down against him through his lips, as she was still balancing on one knee. He pressed right up into her. Dannah went to pull away from him, her mind turning to the hollering she was about to give him. But when he felt her shifting away, Cole wrapped his arms around her waist, pulling her deeper into him.

She gave away her lecture. After another few moments, Cole was the one to pull away from her. "Hannah Marshall, I think I've loved you all my life."

He held her face between his palms and inched toward her slowly. He placed his lips lightly over hers. She felt herself melt into him with no reservations this time. He moved his hand to the small of her back and the other hand behind her bent legs and picked her up.

Cole and Dannah's faces barely parted. She could feel his cheek against hers and his damp breath passing by her ear in slow, shallow heaves. When he set her down against the ground, his hand stayed between her head and the dirt. He only lifted his face to look into her eyes. But Dannah's eyes were closed, so he kissed each lid softly instead. He'd never seen her so calm, so willing to let him take the lead. He loved seeing a side of her that no one else could fathom.

His upper body twisted over hers. Dannah felt a warm draft from the fire pass between the inch of air that separated them. She opened her eyes and pulled him in without a thought of reserve. She felt as though she couldn't get close enough to him. All at once, she was afraid of having to leave this place. She didn't close her eyes again.

Even when she couldn't feel his touch, she felt his breath. And when she didn't feel his breath, she felt his eyes gazing upon her, but then again, she always could.

They lay there quietly wrapped up in each other for what seemed like hours. Only breaking the comfort of silence with a whisper to ask if she was cold or hungry. Cole got up once to fetch some branches from outside for the fire. When he came back in, he immediately lifted her up onto his lap and cradled her again, one arm holding her onto his chest, the other arm wrapped around her bent legs pulling them into his side.

Dannah felt as though every silent night, every whisper in town, every broken bone she'd ever gotten never happened at all. He didn't erase the past; he created her a new one. As if her life were only a calendar made up of those warming days, Fourth of July picnics with drawn out readings of the Declaration, Ring Around the Rosie, and devilish fiddle playing.

Cole felt an overwhelming sense of not wanting for anything. He just was, and this was more than enough. He felt his hairs stand on end just thinking about Dannah, that he was the only person with the ability to see her this way. He was glad of it, too.

They visited the cave many times that summer. Cole's thoughts shrank up and disappeared. He was left with a deep ache for what he had once had, what they had lost. He would be glad if the cave were indeed lost forever.

She was a different person then; she was his Dannah. He had stayed the same, Cole thought angrily. But that was the season before everything dried up in Medea. And before Mrs. Marshall killed Mr. Marshall.

CHAPTER TWENTY-FOUR

When Clare Marshall shot Daniel Marshall, Cole felt a shame-filled burden lifted from his chest, but soon after he found an even heavier heart remained. It was the end of his mother's evil deeds against the Marshall women, and the secret he witnessed could now die. But he realized Mr. Marshall wasn't the first man in his mother's bedroom. A jumble of guilt sat quietly collecting in him, for feeling relieved and for feeling responsible for the devastation of the Marshall family. He felt it slowly filling the deepest tip of his heart, weighing it down like a sandbag across his stomach.

By now the whole town had figured out what his mother and Daniel Marshall had been up to, but Cole bore the disgrace of seeing it, like he was a part of the deception. He felt unsettled and dirty, like he had with Doris.

Cole had heard the rumors of visitors to The Grand, but he had been too young to hold on to what folks were saying for too long. Not to mention, too preoccupied on defending the Edwards' honor and capturing his mother's attention to consider the rumors might be true.

When Mr. Marshall abandoned his ranch, the townspeople hardly knew what to make of the situation. It was the biggest scandal since Mrs. Simpson claimed to have caught the old schoolmistress with Preacher Menard in the rectory.

The blatant confirmation of tittle-tattle had sent them into a frenzy. Daniel Marshall's reputation wasn't flawless, but only because of the oddity of his youngest daughter. He let her work and carry on as a son would have, even before they went through the hard times.

This was all compounded when Daniel took up the bottle and shinnied out on his family. Only had been staying with Mattie for a little bit when he'd been seen around town sick from the drink. Started acting full as a tick, swerving in and out of stores and passing out at the hitching post. They said that Mattie had made Mr. Marshall "unclean" and that he had been a good man, and she was an "infected Yankee whore".

Another time, he was seen kicking up a row in front of the saloon. He was on all fours, barking and drooling like a wild dog. A few men tried to calm him down. But he bit and snarled at them, so they left him in the street to sleep it off or get stamped out by a horse. "One night with

Venus, and a lifetime with Mercury," they'd shake their heads remorsefully.

But Cole guessed Mr. Marshall didn't sober up after all. People said Clare just snapped when Daniel returned. The stress of a woman running the ranch all by herself, dealing with the debts her husband had left. Little did they know, it all fell on Dannah's shoulders. Mrs. Marshall was a shell by then. The Marshall ranch was one of the smaller plots in Medea, after Cole's father had taken over the acreage owed to him from Elisabeth's illness.

Even so, one little girl to tend garden and the herd, not to mention the other animals, it was impossible. They neither had the muscle, the buying power, nor the number of hands to survive. Yes, Cole agreed with the town chatter; Mrs. Marshall must have snapped when she saw Daniel stroll back home again that night. She must have.

Cole finished the last of his canteen, but he didn't go into their cave. He simply pushed on toward his old sod home to figure how he'd cover up the Sheriff's death. The soddy always gave him comfort. It was still used as roundup headquarters. It lay just short of the vast dome of granite that marked the end of Medea.

Cole remembered the old small house vividly where the Edwards had first lived. But after his father built the ranch house, they still went for short stints every so often. His father used to make him dismantle and horse-draw it from plot to plot when the land inspector was rumored to be checking new claims. It was back on its original ground now, and he couldn't help recalling the happiest times of his childhood there.

And just like the cave, he knew the soddy could never be the same, but he couldn't help but wish he'd dreamt the last half of his life up. He had resurrected too much grief for one person today.

CHAPTER TWENTY-FIVE

Around the same time, Dannah was returning from her run-in with Mr. Jeffers and the heifer.

"What did you and Queeny do this afternoon? I haven't seen her this riled up in a long time." Elisabeth was dodging Queeny's tail smacking against her calves, while trying not to step on her.

"Oh, she must have a taste for the forest left in her mouth." Dannah continued restocking the herbs. "Lizzie, how'd you feel about going to visit Grandfather John for a while?"

"To Austin?" Dannah gave a sharp nod to Elisabeth without looking up at her, "No, I should think not," Elisabeth continued, "there's far too much to do around here, plus I wouldn't think you had the time."

"It'd just be you." Dannah said, "I have to stay and get this land business squared away. I'll be expecting a personal visit from the land inspector." She said cheerfully.

"Sister, no. How would you manage without me? There's the garden and Austin is such a long trip."

"Mr. Jeffers is making a trip out there in the next couple weeks. Queeny and I just ran into him."

"No, I can't leave. You're still not feeling all better."

"I'm perfectly fine." Dannah barked back.

"Then why are you scratching so bad?" Elisabeth cocked her head smugly, looking at her chest streaked with nail marks.

"Queeny must have gotten into some poison oak today and passed it off to me." Dannah quickly said, realizing she was still tearing away at her neck.

Elisabeth smugly looked over at Queeny, who had now worn herself into a perfectly sound and still sleep by the fire.

"I'm fine," Dannah replied indignantly. She stopped mid-scratch and returned to crushing up dandelion.

"You know I can't leave," Elisabeth turned and vanished through her mother's bedroom door.

It had only been a couple of days since their Ma had actually laid behind that door, and Elisabeth hadn't yet broken the habit of cutting fresh flowers for her supper-time. Now she did it in honor of her, not for her.

Dannah hadn't thought too much about the night before. In fact, she had felt such a sense of calm and quiet come upon her. She had enjoyed basking in the sun on her private island, and the day felt long, but not tiresome.

The worries were beginning to rush back in, and she felt those familiar sinking feelings that she had grown to live with. She caught herself scratching again. She decided to make her way into town to see what people were saying about old Sheriff Hillard.

As she rode past Mrs. Wilkinson's, she spotted her little girl, Diana, beating out some clothes against the river rocks and slapping them across the washboard. She had grown so fast. Dannah had been there when Diana was born. She must have been nine or so when her pa came running in from the fields and shouted for Mama to head over to the Wilkinson's orchard.

That was just a short time before the Doc had come to Medea. When Clare and Dannah neared the Wilkinsons, Dannah could hear Mary Wilkinson's screams before they had even reached the orchard's edge. She also remembered her ma grabbing Mary's hand and telling her to bite down on a wooden spoon handle.

Poor thing had gone through childbirth six times. She said each one had just brought her closer to death. Dannah believed her, too. Her screams were so bloody, and her face gave it all away.

Dannah had birthed many a heifer since then and felt their chest pounding up through the grass. Watched their big bulbous eyes roll back into their head and waited for them to pop out the top of their skull. But the cows always rebounded fairly quickly and took to their calves straight away.

Mary Wilkinson had a harder time of it with Diana.

Ma said she had been praying for a boy. She had three girls, well four really. One of the girls and the only boy were born dead.

Mama said Mr. Wilkinson needed someone to take over the orchard eventually, and Mrs. Wilkinson knew how disappointed he'd be. Never seemed it to Dannah, though. Dannah felt herself grow a smile remembering the scene. He embraced Diana when they first met, like he'd never let go of her.

But now, she could see something of her mother's disposition in Diana. Something subtle in the way she held herself. In a glance that lasted only seconds, Dannah could see a sense of sadness and of anger. Her mother had never wanted her, and nothing can take that out of a person's bones. It is how they are formed in the womb, she guessed, like a tree root that bends and contorts to get to the shoreline.

The saloon was especially full tonight. Dannah liked when she was able to enjoy the anonymity of drunkards. She found an empty stool at the end of the bar and opened her ears to the chatter, and opened her throat to the whiskey.

By the time she finished her second round, she surmised that Hillard had apparently stripped himself down naked and hung himself. And even though he was without a holster, he held onto his pistol through that attempted hanging. And when that all went awry, he proceeded to shoot himself dead.

And/or he had accepted a bribe from the remaining

free members of the Mexican horse-thieving gang to let their amigos go. They then turned on Hillard, but not before drinking his good whiskey.

And then there was the theory that his wife had caught him with Miss Jane, the oldest and grizzliest of Medea's whores, who then helped Meredith Hillard hoist her husband up over the jailhouse and then shot him. That was the bar goers' favorite.

The theories of Hillard's mysterious magic tricks continued to enthrall Dannah, and the whiskey continued to flow, and the men danced. Every corner of the saloon buzzed with prattle, and impromptu singing broke out every so often. Mostly broken verses of foolish trail songs, and the drunkest of them patted each other as if they were singing to their cattle. Nothing so exciting had happened in a while, but still the town was used to scandal and always celebrated it heartily.

Emily, one of the prettier of Horace Witt's whores, planted herself next to Dannah at the bar, proclaiming herself done for the night. "These bastards are too soaked to remember how to do it and more importantly how to pay me for it. How are yah, Dan?"

She was a grass widow who went by the name Velvet-Ass Rose within the saloon walls and on the line. The line was the procession of wood shanties where the girls lived and conducted most of their work. There was also a back room or two in the saloon.

"I'm getting better by the moment, Emily." Dannah raised her jigger level with Emily while closing one eye and focusing the other in the distance at Henry Edwards in the back.

Horace walked by and jabbed Emily roughly on the side. She rolled her eyes at him. "He's just getting worse and worse these days. The girls say his teeny tiny member forgot to remember." She rolled her eyes backwards again. "And he beats the hell out of us for it."

"So, what do you make of all this?" Emily perkily brought Dannah back from studying Edwards' every move.

"A celebration of sorts," Dannah let go of a triumphant smile.

"Some got more to celebrate than others." Emily gave a subtle nod toward the corner table, where Edwards and some strange men were in the wraps of a hushed conversation. "Official lookin', ain't it?"

"Yeah, a regular town meeting." Dannah gestured toward the barkeep, Roberto. "We've got a lot to celebrate." She insisted to Emily.

"Para el jefe, por favor, Roberto." Dannah ordered a whiskey and signaled it to be sent over to Edward's table.

"Bully for you! You are crazy!" Emily shouted. Dannah turned around in her stool with crossed arms and planted her feet on the ground. She watched poor Roberto shuffle over to the corner with Edward's watered-down whiskey. Edwards swigged it down, looked over at Dannah, and slipped his lips into a tight, sultry smile without hesitation.

Emily, who hadn't lifted an eye from her drink, placed

her hand on Dannah's back. "Honey, he hasn't said a word to anyone all night except those men. He's usually on one of us girls before his ass hits the wood of a chair. But just before they arrived, he just sat in the corner alone, not even drinkin' from his mug, just kept on pulling out his tobacco bag. I'm sorry to say, looks like things are improving for Henry."

"No. He's scared," Dannah hadn't taken her blazing eyes off of him.

"Oh no, honey, he's scheming." Emily insisted. "Who is the next big fat weasel in line for law round here? I'm just glad I won't be paying the Sheriff Hillard tax anymore. If you know what I mean?" Emily nudged Dannah with her elbow and let go of a horsy, wheezy laugh along with a billow of smoke from deep inside her chest.

"Come on Velvet darlin'," a drunken voice came from behind them and snatched Emily up by the waist and clean off her stool.

"A woman's work," she laughed and was gone out the back way.

CHAPTER TWENTY-SIX

Dannah's dreams kept her writhing all night. No sleep would have been far more restful, but exhaustion was cruel, and her eyes fought her and eventually closed again. It dragged her down, sinking her deeper and deeper, until the waking world dissolved entirely. And there she was again. Bound. Helpless and watching.

There she was again, a little brown girl no older than six with long black hair so heavy that it didn't move when she walked, only the cardinal feathers braided into sections of the ends swayed with her movement. She was barefoot and crossing the river.

Dannah yelled to her but couldn't move toward her. Dannah was bound to something, a tree she thought from the feel of the rough bark against her wrists.

The baby girl couldn't hear her over the rushing water,

and the river spilled over onto the shore. She didn't hear the hooves and howls coming either.

She didn't see them until they had surrounded her and stranded her on a little islet. Dannah was writhing, still bound to her bed and to that tree in her dream. Why couldn't she hear her warnings, her screaming?

The pack of dogs lined up on either bank, snarling at her from the shoreline. The little one would find a rock to step to one side of the river, and their barks would grow more and more ferocious, forcing her to fall back to the island. The dogs began to rip at each other's throats, tearing pieces from one another and chewing them up. The little girl began to cry. It was barely audible over the pack. But it was her breathing that floated over the water straight into Dannah's ears, along with the whoosh of the current.

A rider that Dannah can't make out begins to herd the dogs closer together. She yells at him to stop, with one hand free from her bindings now. But the rider is wading in the river. And the little girl finally hears Dannah. She must hear the warnings now, because she's desperately looking to her for help.

The horse's solid frame is halfway submerged, but it is still barreling toward the girl. Dannah's hand finds a pistol at her side, and she takes aim for the rider, who is still faceless. She didn't even realize she was reaching for it until she felt its hard grip in her hand. Dannah can't stop shaking to eyeball him.

She can't tell if she hit him. But Dannah is free from

the tree and sets off running toward the river. The dogs and horse vanish. Just the faceless man holding onto a root on the ridge of the island, his legs straight behind him in a siege of water. The girl again can't hear her, or maybe Dannah's yells are silent. The little girl reaches her hand out to help, but he pulls her in easily. Headfirst, flung over his shoulder like a satchel, but he holds tight to her wrist.

The river appears to be draining like a pail with a hole. He stands up only shin-deep in the water now. The rider pushes the little girl under the water, one huge hand on her forehead and the other upon her fragile little chest.

Dannah finally reaches them, but the rider is gone. She pulls the little dark girl up from below the water, but it's too late. She's not breathing.

She draws her up and into her arms, knees bent up to stop the draining water from taking her away. The palms of Dannah's hands begin to well up with blood as red as the little girl's wet feathers, and the river level begins to fill back up with thick crimson. Dannah lets go; she lets the current carry the little body off.

Dannah didn't mean to let go, but she was frightened by the oozing blood pouring from her palms and filling the river like a freshly dug well. She tried to stop the flow by pushing her palms upon her breast. She pushes so hard. She can't wake up.

All night, Dannah finds herself bound to the tree over and over again. Again, the dogs are coming. She hears the pounding hooves of the rider approaching all night.

Dannah finally woke up from the slight pressure of Elisabeth dabbing at her forehead. "When Queeny was up before you, I figured something was wrong." She wrung out the washcloth in a basin beside the bed.

Becoming more aware, Dannah tried lifting her legs, but it was as if someone was sitting upon them. "Be still, you need to rest. I've got a bit of tonic left, maybe it'll help." Dannah didn't fight her sister's instructions and didn't try to get up again for hours.

Several days passed, but her dreaming hadn't. She felt a little stronger, though. The dreams weren't always exactly the same, and they came to her in pieces. Sometimes Dannah's palms were tied in front and other times she was not bound; she was simply paralyzed with fear. But the little girl's tiny, sweet face was the same, each and every time … helpless and desperate.

Dannah's head still ached fiercely, but after a while, she felt like getting out of the cabin would help or at least stop her from falling asleep again. So she made for the herd with a load of missed chores preoccupying her mind.

Before Dannah left, Elisabeth tried to force some food into her, but she knew their stocks were low, and she wasn't hungry, anyway. Her stomach felt sour, and her mouth carried a very metallic taste.

CHAPTER TWENTY-SEVEN

"Cole!" Billy called to his brother from across the field. He stopped and let Cole mount and ride to him. "Pa wanted me to fetch you. We got to go."

"What is it? Mother?" Billy nodded at him in reply. Cole had thought about that nod so many times, but still he never expected to get it today.

They made their way into town fast, but people must've already seen the Doc rush into The Grand, because no one would look square at Cole or Billy. Just a couple of glances in their direction, but no actual eye contact.

A group of hotel guests had assembled in the lobby, and they abruptly became hushed when the boys walked in. As they reached the top of the stairs, the mumbling came back all at once.

Henry was sitting on the sofa beside Doc Olsen. "How

is she?" Cole asked his pa as he came through the door. Henry said nothing.

Doc Olsen got to his feet. "Won't be long at all. She's been through it all night. It's a blessing, really, Cole. Syphilis isn't a pretty way to go. She's really suffering now. Came fairly fast, too, some people go on like this for years and eventually have to die inside an asylum. A blessing really."

He looked down at his hands as he said it, almost guilty. "Truth is, she may have gone quicker than most on account of the treatments. Some of them tonics she got were expensive fancy things from back east—experimental, more poison than cure, if I'm honest."

Cole remembered they all said the same thing when Mr. Marshall was put out of his misery. People sure had a strange way of making sense out of anything that made no sense.

A violent coughing rose from out of the bedroom. The brothers made their way through the black hallway into an even darker bedroom. "Ma, it's me, Billy."

Cole stood in the doorway, allowing his eyes to acclimate and watching Billy very tenderly take her hand into his own.

"Hello my boys, there's some chocolate on my bureau."

"No, thank you, ma'am."

"Best you'll ever have." She muttered.

Billy stroked her hand. "I know Ma." Cole had never seen Billy be that gentle with anything before.

"You are such a good boy. I remember after I first got

to Texas and I got pregnant with you, all I ate was butterscotches and chocolate. You were bound to be a sweet boy." Billy knew she was talking about Cole, but he continued to stroke her hand and just asked, "Mama, what about me? Billy."

"I was so young and beautiful and so naïve back then." She continued on with her thoughts.

"You are still beautiful," Cole stepped up to the other side of her bed.

"No. This place has turned me ugly, and my youth was wasted here." Her eyes were barely open, and she was tonguing the sloppy words.

"Don't say that. You got Pa and me … Cole and the ranch to show for your years." Billy chimed in.

"Pa. Your pa?" She began to laugh, but it turned into a hacking wheeze that wouldn't quit. Cole and Billy couldn't watch her thrash about in her bed. Billy let loose of her hand and discreetly eyeballed the ceiling, trying to go somewhere else and not listen to the wretched sounds of his mother.

Doc came in when the hacking didn't stop after two or so minutes. Told the boys to help her sit up a bit in the bed; she was basically drowning. She began to convulse with a cough so hard that Henry and Doc had to hold her down from coming off the bed.

And that was it, she was dead. Her coughing stopped, and her body fell limp against their hands that had been holding her down. Her last gasp came as a shock to Cole only because one didn't follow after. It was so strange to hear such a cruel, harsh breath go into her and nothing to come out after it.

It was so unnatural, as though the gulp of air was too much in her at once. The pressure of that final mouthful of air spread throughout her, relaxing her spasmed muscles, and blood began to ooze out from her mouth.

Cole followed the blood spatter from her lips to the blue silk pillow. The line from her final coughing fit sprayed upon her arms and down the quilt. Cole closed his eyes tight.

Billy left for the saloon immediately, said he had to be alone. Henry and Cole sat next to each other on the sofa facing the door without a word between them until the Doc came out of the bedroom again.

"I cleaned her up a bit, Henry. She can stay here till you're ready to bury her, needs to be pretty quick for the hotel's sake though. My condolences to you both." Doc patted Cole's shoulder and left the pair alone in the room.

After a few minutes had passed, Cole whispered, "Sorry, Pa." It was so faint though that the silence remained unbroken.

Henry shifted back against the sofa cushions. "It seems as though my political loyalties are indeed unraveling. Mr. Lusk, the statesman, and a couple of the Rangers were in town to investigate Hillard's death and to appoint a new Sheriff. They couldn't make any promises, until they close the investigation. The Rangers are still looking for those dirty browns that hung Hillard, but they did say I could temporarily appoint someone to take over as Sheriff until things settle down around here."

Cole just nodded, a little stunned from the severe change in subject. It boggled his mind that this seemed more pressing than his mother lying lifeless in the very next room.

"I know you'll be the finest Sheriff that Medea has ever had." His voice got low and demanding.

"What, not me? What about Jeremiah or Mr. Sloane's son?" Cole's voice got increasingly louder and demanding, which apparently angered his father.

He stood up over Cole, sitting on the sofa. "Because you're my son, and people seem to trust you around here, boy. You will do this."

"But the ranch, and we have the Glidden materials ready for the new fence."

"Don't you worry about that. Billy and I'll take care of managing the ranch. This is your chance to put Medea on the map, to be a man. People are watching from San Antonio and Austin, hell the damn Governor's watching. They are watching the land that we happen to be running. If we make a good impression on them, who do you thinks gonna get the pats? Sure, they'll take the credit, but behind closed doors, we'll get their favors. And that's what counts—that is might."

Cole just sat there trying to soak in his father's words. "You just go home and polish up the rifles and get prepared to be a man of power round here, a force. Hell, the very backbone of Medea."

Henry had Cole herded halfway out the door, inching him with his body in sporadic but long strides. He whipped back around. "Oh, your first official business is to vacate the Marshall estate."

Cole stepped forward toward him in anger. "You go to hell." Cole threw his father's hands off his shoulder in shock.

"Calm yourself, boy" he said in a commanding tone, but placed his hand softly and firmly back onto his shoulder, "I know how you feel about her Cole. That's why I felt like you should be the one to help."

"By tossing her off her own land?" Cole couldn't believe what his father was asking of him.

"No, by giving her a fighting chance. She's got a whore's chance at the Pearly Gates of making it through even the mildest of winters. Have you seen the condition of that land, and that lean herd of hers is dwindling fast. She's got family to take her in Austin. I know you want to be the one to save her. But she doesn't want you, Son."

"Don't bullshit me. You don't give a shit about what happens to her." Cole was in disbelief at his father's words. He couldn't take it all in. "You just want every reminder of Daniel Marshall gone. It's Daniel, not Dannah. You are hunting a dead man. But he wasn't the only guilty one!"

Cole cringed backwards a little at what he knew was sure to come his way, but he continued anyway, "He didn't get her sick. She gave it to him, and he wasn't the reason she hated you. That all happened long before Daniel Marshall." And so, it came.

It came down on him like an explosion. His father's swing came with such force that Cole fell back against the door and onto the floor. The door ricocheted off the back of his skull twice before it stopped.

"She hated us, boy, not me," he growled. "You remember that. That land is mine, and she will have to leave sooner than later. Either you listen to me, your father, or I will help her out of her misery myself. You have a week, and I have funeral provisions to make."

Henry stepped over Cole, still stunned and strewn across the floor. "You think you're saving her, but she's already decided she won't be saved. Ever think that maybe I'm saving you from a life of being endured."

He was gone, and Cole didn't dare move until he had heard him get all the way down the stairwell. Cole went to the mirror and wiped the blood from the corners of his lips and probed inside his mouth for a loose tooth by wiggling it with his tongue.

He inched into his mother's room and peered through the door, cautiously surveying the room. It was so still. She looked so peaceful lying there. It was strange to see her so quiet.

He sat on the ground next to her bed. "Mama," he said out loud, but thought to himself, I don't think I've ever called you that. It seemed strange to start now. "Mother, please help me, just this once."

For the first time in his life, Cole really talked to his

mother. Not about fine candies or goose-down bedding, or about her previous life in New York before Henry, but about himself. He knew, of course, that he was talking to himself, but maybe God would be listening closer to Medea tonight.

CHAPTER TWENTY-NINE

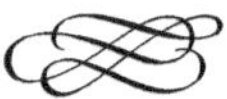

*D*annah made her way back to the cabin with her second jug of water from the river. She usually didn't mind the monotony of fetching water, but today she felt each trip taking more and more out of her.

Still hadn't finished digging the new well. She'd been lucky that the old one had kept so long. A dull ringing still ran through her head, and she felt herself steadily losing balance on Daisy on the ride home, and her eyes burned with glaze.

She nearly came clear out of the saddle once but caught herself with the stirrup just in time. They'd have to make do with the water they had collected from the rains that Queeny hadn't knocked over and the rats hadn't settled upon. Elisabeth would probably still be at the vegetable garden; it was early yet. Dannah dragged herself inside the cabin hoping for just a couple hours of dream-free sleep.

She threw off her hat and stripped out of her damp clothes and headed back into the kitchen toward the warm fire.

"Hello, Dannah." She stopped in her tracks, recognizing the sound of clicking boot heels but not placing the voice. She turned to see a dark figure following her out of the bedroom and into the kitchen. It was Billy Edwards. Dannah instinctively reached to her waist. "I'm afraid all of your personals are back in there, I watched you take them off," He tilted his head toward the bedroom.

"Don't be scared, I just came by for a little chat. We just don't do that enough. Don't you agree?" Billy closed the bedroom door, pulled over a chair between the door and Dannah and slowly sat down on the edge of the wooden seat.

Billy watched Dannah search the cabin floor with intensity. "Oh!" Billy said, slapping his knee. "I put the old girl in the chicken coop, if that's what you're looking for?"

"I hope you don't mind. Figured we all deserve a bit of fun every once in a while. Don't you think?"

"What do you want?" She said over the initial shock of seeing Billy and growing thoroughly annoyed that her plans for sleep had been interrupted.

"I told you; I just need some company." He rested his hands behind his head.

"You remember what happened the last time you came by uninvited?" She let go of a sideways grin.

Billy caressed the side of his head with his fingertips in

an exaggerated fashion. "Aw, but this time, I've surprised you instead, and I have a better view, too."

Dannah was standing in front of the fire in her white dressing gown with her feet spread apart ready to pounce. Just waiting for Billy to let his guard down.

"Besides, I just came by for a little comforting. See, my Mama died today, and I know you just lost your Ma. I thought we could mourn together. Thought maybe you could comfort me?"

Dannah was poised to make a run past him to the bedroom for her gun. She knew he'd be slower than her, but he was big. Billy saw her calf muscles tensing up through her gown and her weight shifting to the balls of her feet. He leaned the chair back on the back two legs and reached his arms in an outward stretch to show that he'd be ready for her charge.

"What? Not gonna say anything?" he said, coming back to the ground again and leaning his elbow upon his knees. "No, 'I'm real sorry 'bout your Ma, dear Billy?" He rolled his eyes in disgust.

A great commotion came from outside. Dannah instantly knew it was the sound of her chickens being pulled apart. It was a horrible sound. But Billy took longer to recognize the source, and Dannah made a swift run for the bedroom door.

He stretched out his fist and grabbed her by the braid as if his big hand was catching a fly. Pulled it with all his might, bringing her back in front of him with a mighty jerk. But Dannah came up on her toes and sunk her teeth into his shoulder.

Bit him with such force that she was sure she'd left a tooth planted in his shoulder. He let go long enough for her to make a run for the bedroom. Billy was left punctured in the kitchen with a handful of her hair.

She found her gun beside her hat and clothes. Billy took his time following her into the bedroom. "Ohh, Dannah put that silly thing down."

"Okay, let me just shoot you first Billy."

"Well, that's gonna be a little hard without bullets." Billy gave his chest pocket a thump, and a 'ching-ching' sound returned.

"Coins." Dannah lowered the gun level to his chest and pulled the trigger.

Billy's grin widened as the empty click echoed through the cabin.

"Damn," he boomed, shaking his head. "Didn't think you'd actually test me."

He dug into his pocket. "You were right, though, wrong pocket," Billy patronized her. "Here, I like to keep things fair." He reached into his pants' pocket and pulled out three bullets. He rolled them one by one toward her feet slowly.

He pulled his gun from his waist and pointed it at her, cocking it with slow, deliberate ease.

"Come now, Dannah, couldn't think I was that stupid? Everyone knows you are a dangerous woman. You shot at me once in the jailhouse, remember? Perhaps, you were just wanting an excuse for me to chase you into your bedroom?"

"Go to hell," she said, still not lowering her aim.

"Oh, darlin', didn't you know? We're already there." Billy swept the door closed with his foot and then took a big step toward her.

Dannah met his step with a swift knee to the groin. But he had gotten close enough to grab both of her wrists, and he twisted her around onto her stomach atop the bed, nearly pulling her arms out of socket in the process.

Her gun fell to the floor alongside the bullets. He tore open the back of her gown, ripped a long strip off, and tied her wrists together behind her. He started kissing down the exposed part of her back. The smell of whiskey came hot across her neck, giving Dannah some hope of overpowering him or at least outsmarting him.

Dannah didn't feel him on her anymore. She realized the noise from the barn had stopped and thought she heard someone come through the door. She yelled out with all her might, taking a deep breath into the shallows of her chest, "ELISABETH, RUN! Run, Lizzie! RUN and hide!"

ole heard her screams coming from the back of the cabin from just outside the doorway. "Elisabeth?" he muttered, trying to catch himself up to what was happening. He was still trying to figure out how Queeny got into the damn chicken coop.

He walked through the disarrayed kitchen and opened the bedroom door to see his brother standing over Dannah, face down on the bed. Billy's foot was hiked up on her rear end, holding her in place. His pistol aimed at the door, which held Cole frozen in place, too. Cole quickly noticed Dannah's dress was torn three-quarters of the way down her spine.

She wriggled out from under Billy's weight and got to her feet, which made Billy smile. He shifted his aim toward Dannah, a far more useful target, he figured.

"Welcome, brother."

"What the hell's going on?" Cole searched the room

desperately for clues and landed back on the pair for answers.

"Dannah and I are spending some time together." Billy waited for Cole to react. "What, brother, are you surprised?"

Cole looked at Dannah, shaking from head to toe like a newborn calf, barely steady on her feet. "Did he hurt you?" He had never seen her like this. She looked terrified.

It almost seemed like the theatrics of one of those plays that had come through town. The chair was on its side on the floor in the kitchen. The woman he loved, half-dressed, with his own brother. "Dannah, did he hurt you?" Cole repeated.

"Not an Edwards' born I can't whoop," she said, not looking at either one of them, but rather straight down.

"Why are you here, Cole?" Billy said with that same huge sneer. "Dannah, are you cheatin' on me with my own brother?"

Cole made a hesitant reach for his revolver. "Don't even think about it." Billy cocked his Colt. "You don't believe me, brother?" He took a step toward Cole. "You think she still wants you, don't you? he laughed. "Could never be me she loves, right?" His laughing stopped.

When no answer came, Billy pushed harder. "She could want me brother. And you're not the only one with secrets, Cole. We all have secrets, right Dannah?"

Cole looked down at Dannah. He could see anger and frustration building up in her. He sensed her helplessness coming to the surface.

When she saw Billy looking intensely at Cole, she turned to look out the window, squinting and searching. Cole watched her curiously, sweeping one foot slowly along the floor and underneath the bed in delicate circles with her toes.

"For instance," Billy was still talking, "Cole ever tell you he knew about your daddy and our ma a long time before he left you all?"

Dannah froze from her strange circles and looked up at Cole. But Cole looked away and stared straight into Billy. He didn't hesitate this time, taking aim at his brother's chest.

"You may get one in me, but I won't drop till she's got a bullet through her head, too. I know how much that'd tear you up inside, losing three people you love in one day," he motioned toward Dannah. "The funny thing is, brother, none of us ever loved you the same. But you …" Billy took aim back at Dannah. "you're my blood!"

He drew in a long, hard breath. "Why her, though? I mean, I can see the appeal, but she's a used-up whore, good-for-nothing but more use." He took a step toward Dannah and took down a strap of her gown with the barrel of his pistol. Dannah spit on his right cheek. Billy didn't flinch. He took another step toward her.

"Billy, just leave and sleep it off. You are out of your mind boy." Cole let the flippant plea fly, even though he knew it was a vain attempt.

"You think it's just the drink talking, don't you, Cole? She's innocent. I bet she hasn't told you neither." He stepped next to her, shoulder to shoulder, grabbing her by the arm and placing her in front of him. He raised the gun to the back of her head. "Tell him!"

"What the hell do you want me to say?" Dannah elbowed him in the stomach, but that too seemed to go unnoticed, which angered her. She was ready to get these boys dead.

"Don't play dumb, bitch, I saw you. I saw what you and he done. I watched him leave my mother's hotel that night, and I saw him stumble in here, feeling his way into your room. I saw you lay with your Pa."

"What the hell! What is wrong with you Billy?" Cole asked, disgusted.

"Tell him!" Billy repeated, getting louder and louder, "Tell him what really happened that night your daddy died." She began to tremble again but said nothing.

Cole watched her eyes flick between the two of them. Her knees buckled, but she didn't fall. Her fists unclenched, fluttering helplessly like wings against her sides.

"I got secrets, too. Hell, I even saw your mama pull the trigger. While he was still on top of you. Crazy son of a bitch thought you were her. Kept calling you Clare, I'm sorry, Clare," Billy mocked, "So sorry Clare".

Her head tilted, just slightly. Her body twitched. Cole could see it. Something was shifting beneath her skin, like a memory working its way out of her bones.

Cole looked toward Dannah, who was just shaking her

head. She finally whispered, "It's true, but it was Lizzie." She hung her head low to her chest.

"Stop lying whore, it was you! I saw you, I heard you cryin'."

Silence. Billy didn't speak. Cole didn't move. Even the wind seemed to leave the cabin.

"Dannah," Cole stepped closer and then hunched backwards a bit to try to look down into her eyes.

"Dan?" His voice was soft now. Not angry. Not confused. Soft. He was trying to pull her back from wherever she had gone.

"Elisabeth's dead. She's been gone long before your daddy was shot." He was still trying to make her look at him with his voice, "Dan?"

Maybe she was trying to pull something over on his brother, Cole thought. Billy kept talking over Cole. "You was hollering out for him to stop. Even promised him you wouldn't run your damn horse so hard, and you'd take better care of your Sunday dress."

At this, Dannah fell back into Billy's chest, eyes flushed back toward the sky and slid down him like a wall.

Her mind was racing, but she felt her breath and her heart stop all at once. She was remembering everything—the night that Billy spoke of, Elisabeth getting sick when they were still little girls, but her never getting better.

Pieces here and there, flashes of her and Mama in the house alone, and those silent nights by herself, not eating, not sleeping. The ringing returned to the very back of her skull, but this time it wasn't low and irritating; it was hot at the surface and seeped in from her eyes, her ears, her nostrils, from the dry corners of her mouth. It was all rushing back to her, and it was drowning her.

She felt Billy's feet make contact with her side. "Lying bitch!" She felt the sharp, stabbing pain; it brought her mind back to the bedroom.

She turned her head to look into the black void that underneath the bed offered for a moment and saw the silver flash laying there, waiting for her. The cabin went silent.

The shot rang up from her gun, and Billy collapsed on top of her. She was too weak to move him off of her. She surrendered to his weight, and her muscles relaxed from their straining. Her grip loosened on the pistol that was jammed underneath them both. She let him lay on her, and she lay still, too. Now, just for a moment, she thought.

"Oh, Jesus! Jesus!" Cole ran over and pried the gun out from under them and slid it underneath the bed. He heard it clank against the hideaway storage frame, and another bullet rolled out from the dark. It sat right on the shadow that the edge of the bed created.

"Oh, Jesus," he repeated, pulling Billy back flat on the floor. Cole tore the blankets from the bed and rested his brother's head on them. He tilted Billy's face to the left and wrapped the last unbloodied blanket around his skull. Half of his damn face was shot off. There was so much blood.

He was still alive, though barely breathing in sputtering, shallow gasps through one side of his mouth and spitting blood out the same side when he exhaled.

"Get more blankets!" He yelled at Dannah but got no answer back. He quickly looked behind him. She didn't move. She was lying on her side facing the wall with her knees folded up into her stomach and her back to Cole.

Her bare spine displayed a bloody, splashed pattern. She wasn't moving at all. "Dannah, go!" he commanded, but didn't hear her get up.

"The devil," Billy sputtered his last thick liquid words, and his head fell toward the side still intact. Cole continued to wipe the blood away from one side of his eye socket and the corners of his mouth for a good while longer until all the sheets and blankets were completely saturated.

Cole fell back to his knees, sitting upon his feet against the bed. The dripping wet ball of his shirt was still clenched in his fingers. He wiped his other palm clean on his bare stomach, which was seizing uncontrollably.

He began to weep, a desperate mournful howl, pity-filled and loud. He slowly made his way on all fours to the other broken body that lay in the room. He slid to the other side of her. Dannah was just staring straight into the wall.

He grabbed her face in his hands. "Why?" He pinched his fingers hard into her jaw and felt her teeth clenched tightly inside. "Why?" He howled.

She said nothing. She didn't even look at him. Her eyes didn't move. When he let go of her head, he shoved it back down into the floor and hard too, he realized hearing the 'thud'. When he felt wet pool between his fingers, he frantically felt for the wound. When Cole couldn't find one, he knew it was his brother's blood in her hair.

Cole did find extremely deep scratches down the side of her neck and a large section of missing hair at the nape. He pushed her braid back to examine the scratches more closely, glancing over at his brother's body just five feet away in utter perplexity. He studied the room again for more answers.

When he recognized part of his brother's ear, the lobe, by the door, he shut his eyes tight, so as not to see any more remnants scattered around the room.

He picked Dannah up and placed her on his lap, scooting as far away as he could into the corner. Facing the wall, he held the right side of her head with his open hand—the side that his brother was now missing. He began to rock in violent sways.

She didn't move. He could barely hear her breathing, and she was so hot. She never closed her eyes to sleep, but she was somewhere else.

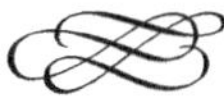

CHAPTER THIRTY-ONE

Dannah didn't go back. Not to the cabin, not to the blood, not to the broken thing she had become. She had left the bedroom. Escaping from Medea, Dannah rode the river's current. She let it carry her soul out and away from herself. Maybe she was going south to Mexico or going toward the coast to see what the ocean looked like. A hand slipped into hers—small, warm, familiar, it was Elisabeth. They were back among the thick ash junipers and cedars once again. Before everything.

Dannah squeezed, holding tight. Afraid that if she let go, the river would take her under.

"Guess what, Dan?" Elisabeth's voice was light, full of laughter. "Ma said she was gonna make apple cobbler for Pa's birthday. Did you know cobbler was George Washington's favorite food?"

"No, Lizzie, I did not. What else don't I know?" She humored her sister.

"Oh, lots!" She took in a huge gulp of air. "Ummm, did you know he had wigs for every different occasion?"

"Let's stop here. Just for a few minutes." Dannah threw down her satchel and pulled her boots off. She was down to her bloomers before Elisabeth could protest. She made her way to the edge of the rocks at the side of the falls.

"Well, come on. One!" Dannah beckoned Elisabeth over.

"No, it's too high, Dannah." She took her shoes off and peered over the lip of the box canyon to the forty-foot falls pouring over.

"We'll do it together." She grabbed her sister's hand and pulled her to the edge. "Two."

"Wait, my clothes!"

"If you don't, you'll have to walk home from up here. Through the woods. Alone. And it's getting dark." She paused a moment to let Elisabeth's imagination take hold of that scenario. "Trust me, sister. Three!"

Dannah whipped Elisabeth's small form forward by the arm, over the edge, and followed behind her. She would never forget the giggle Elisabeth sent soaring that day, when she broke the surface. It was a wet, half-choking laugh, but it was full of life.

"You big bully!" Elisabeth dog-paddled to shallower water and waited for her sister to leisurely float in on her back, spitting water upward as she went, like a horse tail.

"Thank you." Elisabeth said sincerely. Her sister was always there to push her to do things she wouldn't on her own.

"Dannah, I think I want to marry Cole Edwards," she said, barely having caught her breath. "Wouldn't that be wonderful? You two are already the best of friends, and you would be brother and sister. He's wonderful, isn't he? I mean, unless you want to marry him?"

"Don't be silly, we're huntin' buddies. We're too similar. Besides, ranchers don't have time for makin' cobbler and all that nonsense."

She sighed, tilting her face up toward the sun. "I'd bake cobblers every day. Apple, blackberry, peach… Maybe I'd even try that chocolate kind Aunt Mari talked about."

Dannah let herself smile, closing her eyes against the dappled sunlight.

Elisabeth was always making plans for a future she'd never have. And Dannah let her.

"Will you have a big wedding, Mrs. Edwards?" Dannah said, still tickled at the idea of sweets every day.

"Oh, no, just the family." Elisabeth continued.

Dannah continued to float in the shallower end of the pool, letting the water support her whole body and feeling the sun wane in and out of the treetops overhead.

She listened to the gulping sound of the water surging in and out of her ears as her sister made her big plans for their future. She couldn't help but smile every time she heard Elisabeth name a different flavor of cobbler she promised to make.

Dannah didn't come back to the bloodied room; she stayed at the river with her sister for a long while.

CHAPTER THIRTY-TWO

Cole watched as Preacher Menard threw a handful of dirt on top of his mother's coffin and then atop his brother's coffin with just a step. He had not planned on his mother's burial having a companion. All the townspeople felt terrible for him, of course, losing his mother and shooting and killing his own brother that very same night. There was only so much a poor soul could take.

They all seemed to understand it was just an accident, of course, but even so, he stood alone. People believe in luck and misfortune as much as they do booze and guns.

Cole told the story the way a man recites scripture—smooth, certain, unshakable. He explained that he was only trying to shoot the coyote, but the bullet went straight through it killing his brother. It was a horrible turn of events indeed. Coyotes weren't aggressive, just filthy scavengers really, but this one wasn't so easily scared off.

The same cayot was believed to have hit the Anderson's barn last week and brought down a newborn goat, and apparently, he had also gotten into the Marshall's chicken coop completely wiping out their entire flock. Once an animal sees the lazy prey that a farmhouse offers, it gets a taste for such an effortless meal.

Cole had a hard time talking about what had happened. The newly appointed Sheriff Edwards had been trying to save his brother's life. Two tragedies in one day for the poor boy; it was too much.

He said if he had only gotten to the riverbed sooner, heard the commotion earlier, maybe he could have saved his dear brother. Billy must have gotten drunk and stumbled to the river. Everyone saw Billy at the saloon hitting the whiskey real hard after his ma passed. Lots of folks felt bad because they had bought him a drink or two on account of Mattie and all. As Cole recounted the story, Billy must have passed out, because when Cole found him, the coyote was attacking his face.

The townspeople knew Cole, and it was most certainly a tragic accident. But it was evident to them all that Henry Edwards was suffering from a broken heart, too. He didn't even look at Cole during the funeral.

He stood beside the coffins, his face carved from stone, his hands clasped so tightly they had turned white.

The town called it grief, but Cole knew better.

Henry wasn't mourning. He was calculating.

Postmaster Roberson even pulled Cole aside to say, "You know son, grief is a hard battle. Your Pa, well, sometimes it's easier to place blame than to just plain let yourself hurt."

In reality, it had taken Cole a while to get Billy to the river. First, he had to track down a coyote, which wasn't too difficult; he knew just where to go. Dannah and he had found many of their dens. After he got Billy to the river, he just had to wait for someone to happen upon the scene.

He changed his plan a thousand times as he waited. He'd run for help to the closest ranch or pretend that Billy accidentally shot himself, but it was done. After all, he had become law by coincidence or by circumstance, but he held the badge either way, so people would have to believe him, or so he hoped.

No one would understand the truth, and his father would have Dannah on the hanging tree and not just tucked away in Austin, if her name were attached in any way. He'd rather not risk getting caught in a detail of a nearly true story, so he took her completely out of the equation and hauled Billy out of the Marshall's cabin.

As Cole carried his brother's body to the riverside, he found himself pretending that he was simply hauling tools. He couldn't process anything that happened, or that Dannah believed that Elisabeth was alive. Well, that was just crazy. From time to time, Cole remembered Elisabeth as if she had never left. He even recently had thought of her in the Marshall's chicken coop, but those were just drunken daydreams.

Cole had stood beside Dannah and her parents at Elisabeth's funeral. Dannah and him had many talks about how quiet the house was with Elisabeth gone and how sad her parents were. Why now did she believe her sister was alive? And how was it that Mr. Marshall could have possibly raped Dannah? He had treated him like a son. He knew Mr. Marshall, how was it possible that he got so sick in the head?

He left Dannah on the stripped-down bed, in shock or entranced; he wasn't sure which. She smoldered with fever, but he knew he couldn't involve the Doc on this one. So he let her shake, covering her with some coats he found in her parent's chest. He had to risk that she would snap out of it.

CHAPTER THIRTY-THREE

Cole's head continued to spin with questions that she wouldn't want to answer. Was Billy right? Had her father attacked her the night he was killed, or was Billy drunk and causing trouble like usual?

No, Dannah had said it was true, but she had said it was Elisabeth. Cole made his way down past his outer pasture and over the escarpment to the Marshalls' cabin, ready to unload his mind whether she cared to answer or was even conscious. He was bound and determined for the truth.

The cabin felt so vacant to Cole. It was haunting. Her room was empty; she was nowhere to be found, and for that matter neither were Daisy nor Queeny. After a little searching, he came upon her at the nearby riverbed with a knife perched in her teeth. She was holding Queeny between her thighs on the ground. Both girls were soaking wet. Dannah was sawing out clumps of blood-stained fur from Queeny's coat. She was putting up a half-assed fight; normally, old Queeny would have put up a fierce struggle. She must have been still bathing in the glory of her kills, but Cole thought she actually looked guilty.

Dannah stopped and set Queeny free from her grip. He sat down cross-legged next to her. Queeny shook off violently, wetting down Cole pretty good.

"She's a wreck, huh?" he said, not quite knowing the right thing to say.

"You should see what's left of my chickens," Dannah replied.

"You look better," he said, surveying her. "Dannah," he let a thick, heavy sigh go and let his mind stop spinning to release his interrogation. But his tongue landed on the only words he could form: "Why didn't you tell me about your father? Why didn't you talk to me?"

"How could I, Cole? I didn't … I didn't remember it right. I didn't know myself. I haven't done anything right. I'm cursed, Cole." He hadn't expected her to be the one reeling.

"No you're not." He shook his head. "I'm …"

"I heard what you did for me. I know you took the blame." Dannah interrupted, not looking up from twirling her knife from palm to palm. "Told them it was a rabid cayot?"

Cole nodded.

"And they believed you?"

"I suspect so."

"Listen, I'm going to turn myself in."

He tried to shake the horror of last night and the funeral. He straightened his frame upright, now tilting his chin perpendicular to the ground and gathering his composure. "No ma'am, you're not."

"You see, it appears as though I'm the law around here," he flashed her the Sheriff's badge, "And I'm afraid you've already confessed, and I've decided to set you free." Cole had been carrying the silver star in his pocket since yesterday, and he couldn't help but playing with it. Somehow, some sense of power in his life felt unsettling, but fair now.

"Fancy, but ..." She shook her head as if she were drying off like Queeny, "I can't have you carrying the blame for your own brother's death. You don't know Cole, but I know what that's like. I think that's why I went where I did in my head. That's why I done what I did. All this time I thought Elisabeth was the one. It was almost worse not being able to have changed her fate. I won't let you carry this lie."

"That's for me to decide. And I can't have some woman discrediting the new Sheriff's name around here." He flipped the badge inside his hand. He brusquely tried to bring her spirit up again. "I'll do that on my own account, soon enough. We're going back to the cabin to pack up some of your things." He twirled the star in his fingertips again.

"I'm going to take you to Austin, to your grandpa's for

a while. We can ride together or travel by stage." His tone went from confident to quite indecisive.

"No, Cole, I won't. I can't leave." She stood her ground.

"They're coming for you, Dan."

"Soon, I know. You ain't the only one with friends, Sheriff."

"Dannah, just start fresh in Austin, when things settle down here, I'll come for you. Maybe you and I could start up a place of our own." Cole looked toward the ground and turned bright red.

Dannah looked down quickly at Cole's hand as he had placed it on top of hers. "Cole, I'm sick."

"What are you talking about?" He tilted his head and squinted at her.

"I'm sick." She repeated, "No, I'm dying."

"Listen if you don't want to marry me." Cole meant to say the words to be funny, but he realized his feelings really were hurt and abruptly lifted his hand away from her.

Dannah didn't think; she just grabbed his hand and pulled it back into hers. "Doc says I have a while, probably. My father would have, too. Doc says your ma probably had it for a good long while before it got her," she murmured. "But it's inside of me, Cole, and I wanna die with dignity. I wanna die in my home without causing no one else harm. Doc said no infirmaries will take me around these parts anyway."

Cole squeezed Dannah's hand tight. "The pox?"

"After I remembered, last night, it all made sense. I

talked to Doc: the rashes, feeling so weak, and maybe what happened in my head. It's funny how justice works," she stroked the sheriff's star still in his palm. "There's no justice, not here."

She let go of a big, heavy breath. "Or maybe there is, and I just have turned blind to my own doings."

"You're wrong. I know you're not sick." Cole gave her a sweet, slow kiss. A kiss that was so familiar and a kiss that had been missing from her days for so long. Just his lips upon hers. It wasn't like the fire-fueled kisses that they had shared that summer before life stopped. It was filled with love and pain, and it tasted much more bittersweet than she remembered. It filled her up, like blinding tears welling up in her eyes.

CHAPTER THIRTY-FOUR

Cole walked Dannah back home, and Queeny followed behind them, her head hung deep in shame, with splotchy bald patches spotting her coat.

Dannah invited him in for coffee, but after Cole finished his second cup, he didn't leave as he had promised. He had a third and then a sweet biscuit. Then he stayed for a game of cards, but after that he still didn't leave.

They spent the next couple of days together, living as man and wife would. They slept together innocently, but the night had a way of naturally intertwining them. Dannah knew it was Cole reaching for her. The years had made her far too independent, but she was tired now. She didn't fight, and she didn't want to run. She gave way to acknowledging that having Cole next to her made her feel better.

He lay next to her awake, holding her shakes, stopping

her nightmares, and she slept off and on till the dreams stopped each night. He tended to her, and they went to the field together at dawn and worked side by side for the next couple of days, until she grew weak again and had to stay in bed.

She even surprised him one night with a pie. "Why I didn't know you could cook anything but rabbit stew, eggs, and coffee?"

The thought occurred to him around the third day he had been staying with Dannah, that it may be important to show his face in the Sheriff's office. But the parade of deaths seemed to quiet things down inside Medea for the time being.

He had passed through the saloon once and saw his father sitting in the back by himself, but he didn't acknowledge Cole's presence, and Cole returned the favor. He went to get a five-cent shave before returning to Dannah.

On the seventh day of living as a family, Dannah stayed in bed all day, but Cole came home to her that night after wandering around town for a short while and paying a visit to church. She wasn't sure what was happening between them, but she allowed herself to grow more and more content every day. And each night when she woke up to his sleep-softened face next to her, it sent her back into a wonderful rest.

"I brought you something." He pulled a light pink daisy from behind his back. Dannah looked at Cole's mud-stained nails and calloused hands holding the perfect flower up toward her.

She smiled at him and thought of what her pa used to say about being owed a flower for a dance. She took the daisy up to study it. The daisy looked as if it had divided itself down the center. On one side a mass of petals stacked upon each other, and on the other side, an equally balanced semi-circle of oversized but perfectly spaced petals sat.

She smiled, rolling the flower between her fingers. The petals were soft, delicate—so unlike her own hands, rough and calloused from years of work.

Her pa used to say a man owed a woman a flower for every dance.

Cole had never danced with her. Never owed her anything.

And yet, here he was, holding out a perfect, lopsided daisy in the middle of a life that had never given them softness.

She tucked the flower into her dressing gown strap and sat up a bit. "You spoil me so, Cole." She laughed over a stinging in her chest.

"Oh, one more. I almost forgot," Cole yelled, heading back into the kitchen, "Close your eyes. I have another surprise." He peeked his head in and, to his astonishment, she had actually listened and was seated very still with her eyes shut and hands upon her lap. He tip-toed over to her bedside.

Her eyes popped wide open when she felt a lick and a

cold nose against her own. Dannah tried to focus at the pair of black pupils staring back at her from only two inches away. Big awkward paws swung in the air, up and at her face. Cole sat the tiny oatmeal-colored fur ball down upon her lap.

A clumsy paw smacked her cheek. Then another. The tiny creature scrambled back up her chest, its oversized paws making it look more like a bear cub than a dog. He climbed up and scaled down Dannah, biting at her hair.

Dannah couldn't stop laughing. She leaned back against the pillow, allowing him to reach her face, and the pup began licking at her cheeks. She scooped at his rear and held him up in front of her. "So what's his name?"

Cole was taken aback. He hadn't remembered what Dannah's laugh sounded like. "Well, that's for you to tell me."

"How about … Sheriff? Ranger? Cole?" She wiped at her wet cheeks.

"No, he's far too adorable for such a ferocious and handsome name." Cole smiled.

"What do you think?"

"Well, I always thought we'd like the name… I mean if we had…" Cole said eagerly but then came to an abrupt stop. He couldn't remember ever being so flustered. "What about …" Cole picked up again. "No, no, never mind."

"What? Just tell me." Dannah despised not knowing what he was thinking.

"No, it's silly … I just figured we could name it something meaningful. Something from our good times together.

"Like?" Dannah insisted, fully aware of how he had baited her.

"Like when I first realized I wanted you to always be with me as my wife." Dannah looked wide-eyed at Cole. "And when would that be?" She composed herself. She fought the urge to tease him, as she had grown so accustomed to doing.

"Sure, like you don't have any idea," he smiled, relieved at her persistence. "can you guess?"

"I don't think I want to." She poked back. "Let's talk of more permanent things. Things that can be."

"No, it's not sad, it's perfect."

"Um, okay, you want to name the pup, Hunter? River? Cave?" Dannah felt herself blush a bit and then a bit more after thinking about her own confession. She realized she hadn't blushed in a very, very long time.

"Oh no, I loved you long before the cave!" After he saw how red she was, Cole grew braver, realizing he could fluster her, too. It had been since their visits to the cave since he'd seen her vulnerable side.

"Then do tell me, Sir Cole, when did you start with these gallant notions of ever after?"

"Oh, you probably don't remember anyways. We was together pretending to be trackin' or huntin' or somethin'. But really, we was foraging for anything to bring home to your ma, so she didn't catch on that we spent half our days swimmin'. It was so damn hot; it was late August. We happened upon a deer nest near the Kellers' old farm. You remember?" Cole smiled at her.

"You was even gonna let me do the shootin', until you noticed she was pregnant. You yelled so loud; I think the deer in Mexico heard you. I asked you just what you thought you were doing. And you very boldly told me I couldn't shoot a pregnant doe. It was the law and you'd be the one to turn me in, too, and they'd hang me on the spot. We were young, but I wasn't stupid." Cole inhaled sharply and drew out stupid. "I knew you were fibbin', but you couldn't bring yourself to tell me it'd make you sad if I were to shoot her. Dannah, it was easier for you to make up a bad lie and a fake law than to let on about yourself. Hell, if I had noticed she was pregnant, I wouldn't have shot her either. I realized then that I wanted to know the part of you that hollers out without thinking. I wanted to know the unreasonable you. The little girl, not just the little hunter or the little ranch hand." He finally took a pause and looked over at her. "Silly, huh?" he asked, feeling wide open himself now.

"I'm afraid you made her up," Dannah cleared her throat and then said louder, "and that story, too. I'm pretty sure."

"You really don't remember? Isn't it funny what we choose to stay in our head and what we choose to lose completely." Dannah let out an unknowing sigh.

Cole looked into her eyes. "I'm sorry."

"Don't be. All this time, I'd wished it was me instead of Elisabeth. That if it were ... somehow the wounds would be easier to bear than the guilt of not being able to protect her. If I had stayed in bed with her that night and not gotten up or if I had listened harder through the silence…

Well, it turns out it was me. I just wish I'd been the one to pull the trigger, not my Mama. I just can't believe I was so weak that I let him," she said defiantly, "I should have remembered her leaving me. And I should have been the one to kill him."

She stopped and gave Cole a shamed look. "Oh now, I'm sorry," she said, remorseful for speaking so honestly, so harshly about killing. "I just miss her."

"Your mother?"

"No." she shook her head. "Lizzie. I let go of Ma time and time again. I don't think I ever let go of Elisabeth." The words sat heavy in the air. Dannah swallowed, staring at the puppy chewing on her blanket.

"Even when she died, I still went on like she was next to me in bed like when we were little. Read every single one of her books aloud like she would have to me. Set the table for her, heard her voice when no one else could. She cooked for me and Ma, and she kept me company. I don't remember when I truly forgot she wasn't there."

"Maybe she was here for you. Like an Injun spirit you know." Cole said.

"Where did she go then? She disappeared as soon as I remembered what happened. She was in my head. If not, then where is she now?"

"Maybe she's at rest … or taking care of your Ma. I don't know Dannah, all I know is you are back. You're here with me, and I finally get to take care of you." He smiled at his comment, tickled that he had let such a thing slip out like drool.

"Cole Edwards, you ass. I could be blind, deaf, and as lame as Queeny over there, and I'd still be taking care of myself."

It seems during their talk; Queeny had taken to the pup better than expected and almost seemed to be enjoying the view of the pup chewing on her hind leg. She'd never admit to it though. The old bitch snapped at him a couple times with clenched teeth and raised her lip at him, just to show him who was law.

"And what was his name again?" Dannah pointed at the pup dodging from the near nips of Queen Esther. "Deer?"

"I was thinking Augustus. It was in August, always been a good month for us, anyhow."

"You sure it wasn't July?" Dannah laughed. "Well either way, a little Roman Emperor will make old Queeny real jealous for the throne."

"Okay," Cole slapped the mattress and slowly got up from kneeling. "Wanna play some cards?"

"No, I'm feelin' better. Let's go introduce Augustus to the herd," she said, still admiring the two wrestling in the corner, legs atop legs. "I got some haymaking to do, anyway."

CHAPTER THIRTY-FIVE

They tended to the herd, mindfully watching Augustus escape near-death by trampling several times. The herd was nicely contained, and the strays were the usual bunch.

Augustus insisted on ramming up against the cows' legs, like a goat. He must have thought he was their size, and that they were fair game to take on.

He'd prance over to the Herefords, snap at their legs, and scamper away as fast as he could muster. He was so tiny, but still the heifers clustered in a group for protection. They couldn't see him down on the ground from their tight cluster. They just danced around him as he clumsily dodged in and out of their hooves. And Queeny watched over them all, waiting for any opportunity to swat at the pup, almost like she was defending the herd from a terrible beast. She looked up out of the corners of her perfectly circular brown eyes to see if Dannah had seen her outburst at the pup.

"Mind if we ride a bit longer? Daisy hasn't had her legs stretched in a while."

Cole smiled, "No, ma'am," and reared back on Samuel to allow Dannah to take the lead. Cole had Augustus upon his lap. He had tired himself out playing with the herd and was napping serenely in a compact little mound. He bounced like a ball between Cole's thighs and his palm while he rode. Augustus didn't seem to notice much.

All the while, Queeny would run up in front to try to catch Dannah's attention with her sloppy, tongued smile. But when Dannah ignored her sideshow pleas for attention, Queeny would fall to the back of the line, eyeballing Augustus resting comfortably in Cole's lap. Each time she passed back in line, she let her tongue turn into a toothy expression as they passed her.

Queeny continued this charade up and back in the procession until Dannah slowed Daisy down and dismounted at the crest of the hill, wrapping Daisy's reins on the lone oak tree. The same tree she'd watched her mother's funeral from.

They were at the family burial plot just beyond the south bend of the Marshall land. It was where her mother had been buried just weeks earlier, where she chose to forget her father was lying, and where she just now realized her sister had gone before any of them. Cole stayed on Samuel and let Dannah go on alone without a word between them. He cut Queeny off at the pass by turning Samuel's strong legs sideways, creating jailhouse bars.

Queeny poofed down on the grass with a violent nostril-sigh. Cole turned his back to watch the sunset but couldn't help glance back at Dannah walking toward her sister's grave. He wasn't sure if she had realized it, but she had made a sweeping circle around Daniel's grave to get to Elisabeth. He turned back again toward the sunset.

He could see for miles deep within the hillside. He found it curious that the sun chose to shine so brightly upon the shallows of the valley and extend its fingers as far as he could see, but there were some places that it just refused to go.

They weren't really shadows or even blocked by the hillside; it was just as if the land dipped too low and the sun had spread itself too thin along the surface to reach all the way down.

"I'm sorry it took me so long to get here." Dannah whispered.

"I reckon I've gone mad, but I thought you were still with me." Her voice was at normal volume now.

"That you were here. I wish you were. We had fun, right? We took care of each other. At least, I tried to." She peered at the wooden crucifix inscribed with Elisabeth Ann Marshall, 1872-1887.

"I brought you something … I think it's your favorite?"

Dannah took *Alice's Adventures in Wonderland* from her satchel, unwrapped it and placed it upon the gravesite, propped against the cross."Maybe I should have brought *The Adventures of Tom Sawyer* instead."

"I've been re-reading the book about Africa, by Lord… Lord, I don't know. I was thinking we were wrong about them elephants.

I don't think they are dangerous after all. I think they are just clumsy, being such big creatures. I mean, they aren't left with many choices of running or hiding.

It's almost like they have to charge if they are threatened, or their enemy will sense they are really scared. One inch hide or not, if you believe you're fragile, then you are."

The wet wind kicked up. "Sorry for rambling, I thought you'd want to know, I can finally talk to you about your silly books. I read your whole library. Sorry it took me so long."

Dannah stopped and dropped to her knees. "And I'm sorry you've been alone." She stroked the damp grass, like she was running her fingers through Elisabeth's hair. "I wish you'd answer me, just one more time."

She stopped and listened for her sister's whisper, for a bird calling, for the wind to kick again, the swish of the blades of grass, for anything to break the silence. She realized how badly she just wanted to hear her sister's voice say it was okay. But she didn't even know what she sounded like anymore.

After all, she had not grown as Dannah had imagined she had. In her head, Elisabeth's giggle had stayed the same as those days she remembered at the falls. Dannah tried to recall it.

She closed her eyes to picture her face, but she couldn't see it. She had created her in the forefront of her mind for so long. She stored her in that space slightly behind the skin of her forehead, but in front of her skull. She had seen her in the garden, and in the kitchen, or the reading chair, every single day and each night.

But now when she closed her eyes, all she could see were the shapes her cheeks made when she'd smiled, tiny pink triangles. And the blue shadows of her perky nose, but there were no clear images, just shapes. She shut her eyes tighter, forcing the light out from the corners.

She slid down on top of Elisabeth's grave, pressing her ear down desperately to the ground to listen. Still no sounds, only the tickle of grass in her ear. She pushed her weight harder into the grave, imagining herself sinking into it like the African quicksand she read about.

Deeper and deeper she sank, until she was next to Elisabeth, face-to-face in their bed, whispering nighttime secrets, just inches away from each other as they used to do.

Cole tried to focus on the position of the shifting sun that was setting lower. He squinted his face up toward the light and blurred his eyes to see if he could will it to shine where he wanted. Into smooth shapes, it streamed across the valley but still refused to glow at his whim.

He glanced back at Dannah, but she wasn't there. He

saw a tuft of her dark hair rail up in the wind up over the grass and thought it was time to get her.

She heard his footsteps through the ground, but she didn't move until he had almost reached her. He knew she was all right, because her boots were dug into the ground, shifting her body up through her calves into her head against the dirt beneath her.

"Are you okay?" Cole leaned in to grab her.

She was up on her feet and already swatting her skirt off, like she had just taken a little tumble. "I'm okay," She took off for the horses. Cole quickened his pace to keep up with her. He started to veer around where he knew her father's grave was, but she walked right over it this time in a straight path, wafting past his cross, her skirt catching on the left arm momentarily.

She swiftly mounted Daisy, but Cole grabbed the reins and pulled them toward him. "We don't have to leave, Dan. I just wanted to check on you. I didn't mean to rush you."

"You didn't. Don't worry I'll be back soon enough. Besides, too much rest for the children is not good." She looked down at Queeny sleeping like a frog, with her hind legs spread out along the grass, her nose almost touching the little curled ball of a puppy, encircled in high grass.

Cole scooped up the furry creature with one hand. He set him in the crook of his elbow and mounted Samuel with his free hand. Queeny arose with a lax stretch and followed stiff-legged behind them. When they got back to the ranch, the sun was completely gone, but there was no need for lanterns; a full moon lit the way easily.

Queeny raced ahead, presumably for the comforts of a warm cabin, but stopped dead in her tracks, then proceeded to take a drunken stumble sideways, when she realized she had reached the chicken coop. She took off at a trot with her head hung low to the ground.

"It's all right, girl. I'm not mad at you anymore. I understand." Dannah gave her a hard pat on the head as she took off her hat and hung it on the nail beside the door.

CHAPTER THIRTY-SIX

They ate dinner and had the added entertainment of watching Augustus mimic everything old Queeny did, except he had a bouncy spring in his swagger.

Augustus got so excited, he knocked himself clean off his paws and onto his bottom, and his little wind-up tail proceeded to sweep the floor around him clean.

Before dinner was over, Augustus was begging for food just like Queen Esther. He had even acquired the same little whimper, which seemed to annoy Queeny to no end.

Dannah sat by the fire mending the seat of her work pants, and Cole read aloud.

Cole's voice was steady and soft as he read from The Eclectic Reader, *"Two hours from Gérmery was another considerable village; and beyond, the mountains began to exhibit pines of some size, and a variety of smaller trees. At length, the road ceased; and we employed the last rays of twilight with a clambering up a rough and tedious glen, which led us to the top of a mountain ridge, exceedingly narrow and sharp. In the darkness of night, the almost precipitous descent beyond seemed to lead into a bottomless abyss..."* He stopped reading and slammed his book shut. "Are you tired?"

"Honestly, the thought of getting back into that bed makes me ill." Dannah replied.

"Then let's go," Cole stood up.

"Where?" She kept up her needle.

"The saloon," he said, with no intention of taking Dannah into town. There would be too many questions and raised eyebrows and, for that matter, far too many condolences for Cole to bear.

"Next time, old girl," Dannah told Queeny and left her behind at the door to take care of the pup.

"Have you lost your sense of direction in your old age?" Dannah yelled ahead to Cole.

"No, I've changed my mind. Woman, will you just trust me for once in your life?"

"Hell, no!" She stopped dead in her tracks.

"Damn you're a spoilsport. We are goin' swimming."

"Well, why didn't you just say so?" Dannah picked up her heels again and caught up to him instantly. He was surprised at her reaction. She had surprised him many times this week. He exhaled the deep breath that he had drawn in to come back at her.

They reached Hamilton Falls, the point where the

Medea River cascades down over gigantic, smooth rocks, creating clear emerald columns of glass.

"I love this place." She peered over, inhaling a misty breath into her nostrils, feeling the spray come back at her face. She nodded back at Cole in thanks.

"If I were to … when I leave Medea, I will dream of her river forever." She said, peering down into the falls.

"Me, too." Cole said barely getting the words out before laughing.

"What?" she asked, annoyed that he was making fun of her.

"I saw you nekkid here once." Cole began laughing uncontrollably at his deep confession.

His laugh was carried away over the rush of water.

"You pervert!" Dannah felt that strange feeling of a blush coming on again but hid it by sitting down and taking off her boots.

"Come now, you're not a shy girl?"

"I am, too! Never mind that being shy and modest are two very different things."

"I thought you knew. I thought you came here to bathe and to torture me on purpose."

"I sure as hell did not!" Dannah stood up, her embarrassment being replaced with anger.

Cole grabbed her hands and pulled her toward him slowly. "I'm just glad I'll finally be joining you in the water." He said softly in her ear, sweeping her hair back to the nape of her neck.

Cole cockily untucked his shirt and began taking his

boots off. "Just because I've let you sleep next to me in bed, Sheriff," she said, "Sheriff" with particular disdain, "doesn't mean I am yours for the taking."

"Well. I also ate your pie, that should earn me a swim," he flashed her a smug grin, then stuck his tongue out, wading up to his chest in the river.

"Well, turn around." Dannah wanted to punish Cole for his boldness, but she wanted in that refreshing cool water that much more. The sticky air shrouded closely around her.

"Of course." Cole straightened up in the water and faced back toward the falls.

"Yes, yes, always the perfect gentleman."

Dannah knew the odds were Cole would find some way to peek; he had always cheated at hide-and-seek through a reflection or parted fingers. But she never looked up to see if he had turned around.

She took her time undressing. Glancing at the red rashes on her arms and legs that were still visible in the moonlight, Dannah closed her own eyes for a moment.

"You can turn around." She said from the water now.

He let a fake snore break the silence. "Thank you, I must have dozed off." He turned back, sending a little splash her way.

"Will you ever grow up?"

"Probably not. But I got plenty of time to think about it. I think that growing up is something that happens in spite of my best efforts."

Dannah looked glassy-eyed toward the spray of the

falls, that was coming down hard. The river was near the fullest she'd seen it in a good while. "Did you ever know Elisabeth wanted to marry you?"

"Yup."

"How?"

"Oh, she told me once she wanted me to be a part of her family."

"When?" Dannah was so very surprised at his answer.

"I don't remember, in a dream I think. You didn't think you are the only one who got visits from spirits did you?"

"You dream of Lizzie?"

"Or she of me. I'm not sure. But she told me a lot of things, like I was supposed to care for her little sister now."

"Shoot, I guess I don't need to worry about you thinkin' I'm insane anymore." She laughed, but was a bit worried about his response.

"Dannah it's infectious, I think insanity runs rampant in Medea." Cole silently thanked the moon as he gazed at her body through the water.

"I think you should go to your grandfather's." He came back to her face. "If not to Austin, then to San Antonio, I know some people there. It'd just be for a while anyway."

"No." she said, looking him square in the eyes.

"I don't understand. I will come for you as soon as things settle down here. I'll get someone to bring in your herd. We can … we can start fresh, together."

"No." she repeated plainly. "Damn it, Dannah. You don't even have a chicken to your name no more." He broke in harshly, but couldn't help laughing nervously, especially with her in front of him in the water.

He swam toward her. "I want you to be my wife. I don't care that you think you're sick, you look just fine to me."

Dannah sank down, so the water covered her arms; she didn't want him to see her marks. She liked pretending for a moment that something else could be. Cole tried to concentrate. "It's just all that's been going on around here. It can take a lot of a person."

"You just want to lay with me again," she smiled coyly through her words, "I'm afraid, Sheriff, those vines have grown deep over the Cave of Lost Adventures, and I'm not gonna let you take advantage of me again." She sent a splash his way.

Dannah knew Cole wouldn't catch on to her changing the subject. She also knew he'd never accept that she was sick. So she spared trying to convince him again and played along.

He wiped the water from his eyes and feigned shock at her newfound playfulness. "Take advantage of you? You kissed me that first time in that cave." He pointed his finger at her.

"I did not," she barked back. "I was hungry, and you were holding those biscuits for ransom."

"You liar!" He sent a splash at her again. His tone steadied. "Will you at least think about going to Austin? I could, of course, pick you up myself and send you inside that damn dowry trunk of yours."

"I'd like to see you try." Cole took this, of course, as a real challenge and swooped in on her.

"You brute." Dannah couldn't resist a good fight back, and she bit him on the top ridge of his ear playfully. He wrapped his arms around the smooth small of her back. He could feel where the curve of her backside began.

"Oh, you are a wild beast," he said, baring his teeth, but his expression quickly changed when he went to kiss her.

Dannah exhaled, the breath shuddering out of her as the river rocked her weightlessly. She relaxed once again into his arms, and into the River Medea, but this time it was on her own account. She had forgotten how it felt to relax all her muscles at once and enjoy the rocking of the water and the warmth of Cole's chest against her. To let go, to let the water carry her. To let someone else hold her without bracing for pain. The river cradled them both.

CHAPTER THIRTY-SEVEN

He carried her on shore without protest and dried her off with his shirt. They got dressed in silence, but neither turned their back nor looked away.

"If you're sick," Cole whispered, "I don't care."

The words felt strange on his tongue—not because they weren't true, but because they were too simple for everything he was feeling.

He exhaled sharply. "I just want you," Cole conceded. "I'll take care of you."

She said nothing, and they started back in silence. After a while, Cole grabbed for her hand that was swinging in stride by her side.

"I've imagined starting a family with you so many times it feels real. About being your husband, taking care of you, and you maybe taking care of me. I thought about the ranch house I'd build for you and the land we'd work side by side. I want you, Hannah Marshall."

Dannah watched their feet take turns stepping up as they walked and talked. She heard his heart-shaped words but focused on the feeling of his hand holding hers.

By the time he stopped talking, Cole felt completely drained, like he had poured all he had into those sentences. He silently waited for them to wash over her.

Dannah squeezed his hand tightly. He took a moment to breathe again and realize that she was answering him. It wasn't a brush off; it wasn't an accident. No matter if she realized it or not, it was confirmation that she wanted him, too.

They locked eyes for a brief moment. Dannah smiled at him, and they kept walking, trying to relax into the high-toned excitement, this fortune found.

Cole felt her grip release suddenly. Dannah stopped mid-stride, and she lurched forward on her toes and took off.

Cole's stomach dropped.

They were only half a mile or so away from the cabin when she noticed the strange glow in the sky. The wind must have been blowing with them because neither of them had smelled smoke. A trick of the light, maybe. But then she felt it—the faintest shift in temperature, the ghost of heat licking at the wind.

Dannah's pulse slammed against her ribs.

She was running before she even realized it, before Cole noticed the blaze. She didn't slow down for his shouts. He was only a few steps behind her now, but he couldn't catch up. He was astonished at her long, hard strides, and he lunged at her shirttails several times.

She was inside the cabin and rushing through the flames without hesitation.

Cole, however, did pause when he reached the cabin door, his breath ragged and loud.

But he heard a voice soar above from a distance. "Cole!" A voice, cutting through the roar of the fire. His father's. It took him a moment to recognize who it was, because it seemed so out of place. His head whipped toward the tree line, toward the figures on horseback.

Henry took off on horseback from his shelter back against the tree line. Two other men that Cole hadn't recognized followed him toward the cabin.

He regained focus when he heard Dannah screaming for Queeny. He took out his dampened overshirt from his pack and wrapped it around his shoulders and rushed through the doorway after her.

Cole's eyes instantly burned with smoke. He took the sleeve of his shirt to wipe them clear and then turned the shirt backwards like a bandana over his nose and mouth.

The heat pressed against his body, thick and suffocating. He felt the hairs on his arms singe and his skin begin to blister. The flames lapped at the walls and floor. The smoke billowed a shade of black he'd never seen, churning and swallowing everything.

"Dan!" He spun around several times, losing his bearings within the billows of smoke.

"Dannah!" He wailed over and over again, each time searching through the thick drifts of smoke. Every attempt he made to find an open path deeper into the cabin was quickly altered by plummeting beams and flaming thatch falling down on him as the flames popped and hissed.

His head swam with dizziness, and he breathed through a tight burning in his chest. He felt someone grabbing at him.

A figure—movement—something in the corner of his vision.

"Dannah?" he screamed out, but it was only as a raspy whisper, almost like a prayer. He reached into the smoke for her.

CHAPTER THIRTY-EIGHT

When Cole woke up, scattered pieces of wood around the frame still burned with small, shallow fires. But the cabin itself was hollowed; it had been gutted and swallowed up by the flames from the inside out.

At first, there was only the smell. Thick, acrid, clinging to the inside of his throat like tar.

Then the pain. A deep, searing ache radiating from his chest, pulling tight with every breath.

Cole blinked; the world slow to return.

Small fires still flickered weakly around him, dancing over the skeletal remains of the cabin. The air was heavy, full of embers and loss.

Then it hit him. Dannah.

His body lurched before he could stop it, sending a bolt of pain through his ribs. He choked on soot, coughing until his lungs burned. His father was beside him, silent. Waiting.

A terrible, painful cough rose from his heavy chest, allowing smoke to clear from his throat. It left his mouth desiccated. Cole saw his father next to him on the ground. He tried hard to swallow but couldn't find any saliva in his throat or mouth. All he could taste was thick soot coating his tongue. "Where is she?" He nearly hissed at his father. He said nothing. "Where is she?" Cole cringed at the flaring burns across his chest that stretched taut as he tried to sit upright.

"She's gone, son. We think a lantern must have caught on a curtain or maybe the stove plumed up …" He offered his canteen to Cole. He took a huge gulp in and felt ash run down his gullet along with the water. The water was so cool it burned even more than he feared.

"Did you even look for her?" Cole only paused a moment for a reply, but he knew his father would just pretend to be offended. "Why did you even bother saving me? Because you need a Sheriff to do your bidding?"

"What disrespect you show your father. I made you, boy." Cole heard a whimper over the crackling.

He jumped to his feet. He looked at his father sitting on the grass and gathered all the moisture he could in his mouth and spat it down upon his face. He bent back down into the weeds, grabbing at the shiny silver sheriff's badge that had fallen out of his pocket. He left his father kneeling beside his canteen and headed toward the chicken coop that was still intact.

Cole scanned furiously. He found Queeny licking on Augustus, just shy of the ring of smoldering fires.

He reached toward Augustus, moving his fur aside. Queeny kept on licking around the scruff of the pup's neck. He could barely see in the dark of night, but Cole's fingers felt bite marks under a singed patch of hair.

He picked Augustus up for a closer inspection and, except for a charred tail and a sopping wet throat, he seemed to be fine. As soon as Cole put him down again, Queeny went back to licking at his neck.

Cole noticed Queeny's skin was scorched raw, especially in the bald spots Dannah had cut out earlier that week. He turned back toward the cabin. Stepping over the smoking heaps of rubble, he looked for any signs of her. A sinking feeling told him there would be none. He picked up The Eclectic Reader, which was badly blistered, and gathered the scattered pages, placing them in a stack.

He wandered around in circles, finding more loose pages, a photograph of Mr. and Mrs. Marshall, and a left boot. His stack was becoming a mound. Soot, soot, and more soot. A flash of pink caught his eye among the sea of black ash. He knelt, brushing the ash away, his fingers closing around the brittle remains of the perfect pink daisy. The last thing he had given her. He swallowed hard, tucking it carefully into his pocket like a relic.

He straightened, but he didn't move. He just stood there, staring at the ruins of the cabin, at the smoke rising toward the sky. Dannah was gone.

CHAPTER THIRTY-NINE

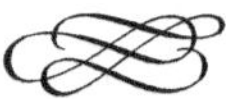

Cole spent the night going through the rubble for her remains and for anything worth remembering her by. His salvageable pile was large, but all insignificant except for the daisy. The moon was not nearly bright enough after all.

He finally laid down just on the outside of where the cabin wall would have been, just shy of the lines of ashes. The dogs lay butted up next to each other. Curiously, Augustus had rebounded from the shock fast and had switched roles with Queeny as nursemaid. Cole noticed he frequently got up to circle Queeny like a soldier.

He would get up to her big muzzle, which made them pretty much eye to eye on the ground, then take a timid hop forward and lick her nose or one of her closed eyes. Then Augustus would circle back past her heaving stomach and drop down to her hind legs and nestle in between her paws. Queeny winced every time the pup touched her.

Cole hadn't noticed that Queeny had taken a turn for the worse until he saw her try to get up, presumably to find water or perhaps to look for Dannah. The old girl's legs gave way under her. Where she fell was where they had all gathered to sleep. Cole shut his eyes tighter now, as he pretended not to hear Queeny's heaves.

She wasn't better when he woke up a half hour later; he guessed from her unraveling whimpering. Cole picked her up and started toward the river. The walk was a march. He kept a rigid stance as he corralled Augustus with his feet and hugged Queeny tight in his arms so he wouldn't jostle her too much. He felt the heat from his chest burns go up behind his ears. His knees stayed locked as he manipulated the downward slope of the landscape.

Cole's heel became lodged in a tree root. He tried to step forward and pull his leg out of the nook but came down on one knee with all of his weight. Queeny remained bundled safely in his arms. Cole hung his head over her for a moment and stood up very slowly. His body seemed to work in quadrants. First his feet and shins stiffened, he pulled his waist up and then his chest and head painfully followed. Cole continued toward the banks.

When he got there, he placed Queeny by the river, stroked her head and her long ears for what seemed like hours, but the moon hadn't budged yet.

"It's alright, girl." He repeated over and over in her ear.

Cole studied her ribs—rising like a breath drawn too slow. He couldn't let her suffer that.

At this point, Augustus had taken to stumbling and sleepwalking down on the banks. When the pup made it up shore a ways, he stood up straight and lowered his rifle.

Queeny let go of a soft whimper. It floated above the riverbed downstream. She lifted her eyes slightly to look at him, still trusting.

Cole Edwards shot the Queen in the back of the head. Queeny instantly drained of fluids as her body went limp, and her muscle tension faded.

He quickly turned his back toward her. He saw all four of Augustus' paws come off the ground and his tail tucked under him as he landed on his hind paws.

Cole managed to get his shirt wrapped around Queeny, nice and tight so that only her tail protruded. With a loud grunt, he picked her up. She was so heavy, so much heavier than she had felt just minutes before.

Cole could feel the inside of his eyelids scratching his eyeballs with every blink. He hurt; every piece of him throbbed and burned.

When he got to the top of the hill, underneath the big oak in the pasture, he peered down upon the tiny crosses in the distance. He counted the three crosses that marked where the Marshall family lay at rest. He now had the Queen dead in his arms and his Princess dusted upon his soles.

All at once, Cole felt undone with a deep lightning bolt of longing and despair. It rushed through him like a current. He felt like all the marrow was being sucked clean from his bones. Slowly, his insides went dry, like taking in the last sip of a cup when the slurping sound commences.

They felt like they drained from his wrists, then from his shoulder blades, and up from his thighs. Cole's frame went hollow as he felt his entire body shrivel into one jelly lump. Everything he had came together into his stomach, making him nauseous. Making him ache right at the lowest point of his belly, right above his groin. He swallowed the sick feeling further down.

As he began digging her grave, the moon still shone, but by the time Queeny was buried the sky had finally begun to lighten. He threw the last shovel of dirt back on her and began to pray.

"Our Father" Cole muttered, "who art in Heaven…" Cole finally released.

He dropped down to his knees in sobs. Rocking back and forth from his toes to his knees and collapsing forward again to vomit. His cries became moans, and his moans eventually became gasps for air. Cole crawled back up to the shadows of the tree. He was out.

The searing sun woke him, hot on his already blistered cheeks. It took him a second to realize Augustus was lying on his bare chest. He only noticed the little ball, because his burns were stinging so intensely. He set him carefully down on the ground next to him and watched him whirl about in circles before plopping down on the grass and heaving a grunt Cole's way.

Cole let his eyes strain against the early afternoon light. He let the memory of the night, of his past month, roll through his head like he imagined them all—as if Dannah had never left him.

Cole got to his feet and inched his way toward the field, waiting for Augustus to join him. He paused at Elisabeth's grave for a moment. He wondered if he could live without her. Would Dannah visit him in dreams as Elisabeth had, and could he bear her to? Would her soul be at rest for all she endured in life, or would she be a ghostly prisoner here in Medea? Cole peered down again at Elisabeth's grave and noticed something peeking up through the grass. It was a book; he snatched it up.

Cole smiled when he saw it was Alice's Adventures in Wonderland. He ran his fingers down the ripped spine and thumbed the pages. He opened the loose-leather binding up and read the words printed in Dannah's handwriting on the inside cover, *Property of Mrs. Hannah M. Edwards*.

For a moment, he laughed. He expected to see Elisabeth's name, as he had noticed on most of her books. His head began to throb through his ears. His chuckle turned into a painful ache that traveled deep into his toes.

Somewhere inside, she had known reality. And she inscribed their reality with his name. Dannah had indeed loved him always. What Cole felt before in her eyes had been true; he had not made it up. He had looked into her.

Not the little girl, not the little hunter or the rancher; he had known Hannah Marshall. The woman that was supposed to exist, but he'd been the only one to know it.

Years had passed since Cole and Dannah had forged the wilderness together as the best of friends. Cole recalled the moments that changed everything for them in the Cave of Lost Adventures, when the outside world was washed away. Cole remembered how he felt inside the infinity of those moments. Time stopped forever for Cole and for them as a couple, as an us.

He could see her face perfectly now and her dark wavy hair flowing down. He knew their moments were all in the past. They were carried upon the winds that skimmed the top of the Medea River. He was broken. What had been written for him died with her.

He pulled out the mangled pink daisy from his pocket and pressed it inside the book. He tucked the book deep down inside his pack. "GO!" he yelled suddenly at Augustus.

He pointed in the direction over the hill toward where his old soddy lay. "GO!" Augustus looked up at Cole, very startled, but he didn't make a move. Cole shooed at him, crying now. "I'm not fooling. Go that way," he growled.

Cole picked up his sack and turned his back to the pup. Augustus didn't move at first. But when Cole looked back, he had gotten up to follow. Cole ran back at him and kicked him, sending him flying back to the ground where he started. Cole didn't look back this time, and Augustus didn't follow.

He made his way back to the river in a short time, pulling the book from his pack before his feet were wet. He slid the flower out of the pages and threw the pack on the banks. He plucked the remaining petals, and one by one released them into the current.

He let the book go next, but it bobbed about on the surface clumsily. The petals had merely laid across the surface and danced down the river. The book of Alice had been trapped spinning and drowning in the water, too heavy to dance, too light to sink. He took a step to retrieve it, but it slipped down into the mud. When he recovered it and himself, he removed his rifle from across his back and held it over his shoulder. He stared deep into the water.

The river seemed to slow down, but the current pulled just as strong. He looked upon the surface, which appeared as one delicate sheet. He wondered if his body would act as the petals had and carry him out of Medea gracefully or would he writhe around painfully as the book had?

His thoughts turned to her—to joining her and to becoming untouchable together. He sunk to his knees, submerging his head back into the river and kept that stance until he started to choke and cough from the water rushing in his nose and mouth. He tried again but broke the surface coughing and hacking. He wedged his rifle between two large rocks at his feet and once again went under. He held the center of the barrel, pulled himself down, and waited for his air to run out.

Something unusual caught his eye, a flash of silver

near one of the rocks. It didn't belong there. He kicked closer, struggling against the current. It was the sheriff's star. It must have fallen out of his pocket when he slipped.

Cole looked upon the silver star, which seemed brighter than before. Five cruel points. He held it like a mirror and, for a moment, didn't know whose eyes were staring back. Not Cole, the boy. Not the son. Not the lover. He felt as though a stranger was blinking back in his place.

He felt a sudden rush of fear enter his body, and the urge to retreat overwhelmed Cole. He pinned the badge to his belt and departed the water. The law had never saved him. Never saved her. But here it was, refusing to be buried.

He pulled the book from his waistband and opened it up once more. The ink with Dannah's real name was almost completely gone from the inside cover. He carefully wrapped it up and placed it back inside the pack.

Augustus was not far from the spot where he had left him. Cole walked to Augustus and patted his side. He made sure that the pup knew it was okay to follow, and Cole glanced back every couple of steps to make sure that he was.

The pair made their way toward the very first home Cole had known, the old soddy just short of the vast dome of granite that marked the end of Medea.

He thought of that old river song his father used to hum. About a horse that couldn't swim and a man who beat him, anyway. He felt like that horse now—half-drowned and dragged along, spurred by grief instead of leather.

They disappeared into the prairie where the soddy waited—two shadows against the ground. It wasn't much, just a hole in the earth, with a roof made of time. But it was theirs in the end. A man, a pup, and a ghost for every corner. In Texas, that was how it ended. A hell of a country for men and dogs, but just plain hell on everything else.

Oh, I came to the river
And I couldn't get across;
I paid five dollars
For an ol grey hoss,
I put him in the river
And he couldn't swim;
So I gave him hell
With a hick'ry limb.
I spurred him in the shoulder,
I spurred him in the flank,
And you oughter seen the sucker fish,
A-swimmin for the bank.

— COWBOY SONG 1830, AUTHOR
UNKNOWN

EPILOGUE

ire leaves nothing. Don't be entranced by its flicker. Fire is ugly, brutal, and barbaric.

Smoke swirled like phantoms among the ruins of the Marshall's cabin for days. Where long ago, Cole remembered a full home, brimming with giggles, bursting with beautiful dancing and joyous celebrations—there was no one left. No voices rose, and the ashes told no lies.

The hollow wind blowing through the prairie grass reminded Cole of how fast they'd traveled from this earth without a thought of leaving him.

He would never return to the Marshalls' land. That life was gone, along with Dannah, his brother, his mother, and the last traces of the boy he was.

Instead, he stood in the middle of Medea, nestled close to Samuel, watching the players circle around him in a dance. A carnivorous ritual—neither mating, marrying, nor marauding interested Cole. All of the mundane motivations of life in Medea left Cole feeling one of two ways: numb or disgusted.

Cole watched from his shaded stoop in front of the jailhouse as his father, Henry Edwards, stepped out of the saloon.

Henry paused on the boardwalk, lighting a cigarette with a slow, deliberate flick of the match. He stood there a long moment, studying the street as though weighing something unseen. Then his gaze slid toward Cole, sharp beneath the brim of his hat.

Cole met his eyes. No words passed between them, but something did. A recognition. A warning. A question left hanging.

Henry gave a faint nod—barely there—and turned, moving off down the boardwalk with a purpose that left Cole uneasy.

The jailhouse didn't feel like home, but Cole savored how people kept their distance, from it and from him.

They whispered, of course. But now they looked at him like he belonged here. A man carved from ruin.

He wore the badge; for now. He didn't want it, but he couldn't stomach the thought of who might take it if he didn't. The kind of man who'd step up for this honor was exactly the kind who couldn't be trusted. A huckster. A puppet. A maniac. Cole wasn't sure what that made him on any given day.

He took the badge like another man might take a bullet, and carried it like a shield against the wreckage of his world.

BURY MY NAME

THE COLE EDWARDS SAGA — BOOK ONE
FOLLOW-UP TO THE DAISY CHAIN

Also *From Death Do We Party Press*

Cole Edwards has lost everything. Dannah is gone. Billy is dead by his hands. And the town of Medea is smoldering in the wake of its sins. Forced to reckon with his past, he wears the sheriff's badge, but his hands are still stained with blood.

When new dangers creep into Medea—a roving band of the last vestiges of Comanche resistance attacks homesteads from the north, outlaws testing the limits of law, and a woman who threatens to pull him from his grief— Cole must decide: is he truly the law, or is he just another outlaw waiting to be buried?

His father, a reprobate who treats him less as a son and more like property, still angry about Billy, and determined to get his pound of flesh for his protégé's untimely death, pushes him to his breaking point.

In a land where justice is written in blood, the past is never truly dead.

And neither is Cole.

Coming Soon…

Shop books, exclusive merch, follow our socials, and access additional free content

WEST OF NOWHERE

THE AETHER GUN — ASHES & DESIRE
BOOK ONE

A NOTE FROM ERICA M. GOROS

If you enjoyed the grit and emotional intensity of The Daisy Chain, you won't want to miss West of Nowhere. Though different in genre, both stories share a world where love is tested by violence, where survival is never guaranteed, and where the past refuses to stay buried. This is a story of war and consequence, of desire and destruction, of two people who should have never found each other—but did. And now, neither of them can turn back.

Some loves survive the fire. Others are made from it.

Shop books, exclusive merch, follow our socials, and access additional free content

THE WESTERNERS

AN AETHER GUN STORY

In the West, even silence has a cost.

In the shadow of the Davis Mountains, fifteen-year-old Emory Cade's quiet life is shattered when her brother vanishes as the Texas National Army is taking over the town. What begins as a desperate search for family leads Emory into a world of secrets buried beneath the desert stone-where soldiers guard a strange machine and rumors of something called Aether run like wildfire.

Drawn in by a woman who seems to know more than she says, Emory discovers that her bond with her brother is only the beginning of what ties her to the struggle. As reality begins to blur and the lines between truth and illusion bend, Emory must decide who she can trust-and how much of herself she's willing to risk.

The Westerners, prequel to West of Nowhere, is set in the uneasy years before the collapse. It is a mixture of Stephen King's The Dark Tower meets Cormac

McCarthy's No Country for Old Men—a gritty blend of Western survival, military tension, and emerging sci-fi intrigue. A standalone novella that ties into the upcoming larger saga.

The reviews are in…

"The characters just jump off the page!" 5★

"So real, I almost wonder if the author knows something we don't!" 5★

"A story so compelling that it deserves a close examination!" 4★

Shop books, exclusive merch, follow our socials, and access additional free content

WEST OF NOWHERE

THE AETHER GUN — ASHES & DESIRE
BOOK ONE

Also *From Death Do We Party Press*

Jake is no hero, but he's got great taste in women that are...

The country has gone dark. Texas has broken away. But the war is a distraction, and as the opportunistic players set up for their power grabs, something else is moving beneath the surface. Something no one could prepare for.

Lovers Jake & Lys are caught in the subterfuge.

As cities and scoundrels topple, Jake goes barreling toward trouble at every turn. His answers drive him west toward dark secrets not of this world.

In this new land, where pasts and futures collide, love and vengeance walk the same road.

Coming Soon...

Shop books, exclusive merch, follow our socials, and access additional free content

ABOUT THE AUTHOR

ERICA M. GOROS is the author of The Daisy Chain–Prequel to the Cole Edwards Saga, a haunting, heart-split novel of women, land, and legacy in the Texas Hill Country. First released in 2011, the revised and expanded edition of The Daisy Chain marks not just a return—but a reckoning. Erica is the co-founder of Death Do We Party Press, a story-driven publishing collective devoted to work that lingers and loves that last.

Raised in Dallas and educated in Austin, she earned her degree in Journalism with a concentration in Photojournalism from the University of Texas. She's written fashion copy for some of the most iconic brands in the industry and co-founded a wellness company rooted in ritual, resilience, and deep nourishment.

She lives for her three boys—wild-hearted, sharp-eyed, and the best stories she's ever helped write. Most days, she balances book launches and bedtime routines with freelance deadlines and dream drafts. Her voice is shaped by family, memory, and the belief that a good story should never leave you the same.

IF YOU ENJOYED THE DAISY CHAIN – PLEASE REVIEW IT ON AMAZON, GOODREADS, & BOOKBUB

Review the Daisy Chain